Praise for

GIRL ON POINTE

"A lesson in the importance of self-knowledge. I recommend it in earnest."

—EMILY KATE LONG, 4dancers.org

"Picks up where *Girl in Motion* left off, transitioning young Anna from student to professional, from girl to woman and everything that entails."

—Mercer Island Patch

Praise for

GIRL IN MOTION

"I couldn't put down this novel about the ups and downs of life in a ballet boarding school."

—AMANDA BRICE, author of *Codename: Dancer*

"*Girl in Motion* offers an inside view of professional dance training."

—*The Salt Lake Tribune*

"If you want to know what it feels like to be a dancer in vocational training (from a fictional perspective), give this one a whirl."

—BalletNews.co.uk

Praise for

Lauren
in the
Limelight

"The prose is beautiful, and the novel's themes of personal discovery, empathy, friendship, grief, and family dynamics are explored with subtlety and depth. Impossible to put down—even if ballet isn't your thing.

—*Kirkus Reviews*

"This is the book I wish I could have read as a young ballet student."

—MEGAN FAIRCHILD, principal dancer with New York City Ballet and author of *The Ballerina Mindset*

"I so wish that *Lauren in the Limelight* had been in my local library when I was a tween-ager . . . I would have loved loved loved to imagine myself Lauren then and I know that tweens—ballet fans or not—are going to love it now."

—NANCY PEARL, author of the Book Lust series and *George & Lizzie: A Novel*

"*Lauren in the Limelight* promotes empathy and understanding and deals with the crucial moments in life when we gain maturity, break from our parents' version of us, and become ourselves."

—PETER BOAL, Artistic Director of Pacific Northwest Ballet and author of *Illusions of Camelot*

GIRL ON POINTE

Also by Miriam Landis

Lauren in the Limelight

Girl in Motion

GIRL ON POINTE

a novel

M I R I A M   L A N D I S

Rhododendron Press
Seattle

Girl on Pointe

For information about this title or to order other books and/or electronic media, contact the publisher:

Rhododendron
Press

www.rhododendronpress.com

ISBNs:
979-8-9883078-5-3 (softcover)
979-8-9883078-6-0 (eBook)

Printed in the United States of America

Cover and Interior design: 1106 Design

Cover image of Sarah-Gabrielle Ryan copyright © Dan Lao

Typeset in Adobe Garamond Pro

For dancers

Author's Note

I remember exactly where I sat in the winter of 2003 when I wrote *Girl in Motion's* first words. *Girl on Pointe* was originally part of that first book, and I only later split Anna's story into two. The Mirrielees apartments at Stanford University housed approximately 340 students, but I was the only resident who had been a professional ballerina. As a twenty-four-year-old junior, I was older than most undergraduates. There were two other retired dancers in the class of 2004, and all of us had been well into our twenties on our first days on campus. A few days earlier, weeks before taking the MCAT, I'd left the premed track and switched my major from Human Biology to English Literature.

There I was, wondering how I'd gone so far down another career path and why, once again, I was switching directions. I began to write, hoping to figure myself out.

Later, a few years into my editorial career at major New York publishing houses, I realized that an endless number of books originate from an author's sentiment that "no one understands what I've been through." And for good reason—in the twenty years between my writing days at the Mirrielees apartments and this copy of *Girl on Pointe* landing in your hands, I reached a deeper understanding of how unique and mystifying a dancer's journey is.

I had grown up reading every ballet book and watching every ballet film I could get my hands on. If ballet was to be my life—and I knew it was from a very young age—the immersion was about so much more than what I learned in the studio. The book and movie options were slim. There's not much in the media about ballet beyond outstanding nonfiction. You can count on one hand the number of novels written for and about dancers during the most critical training years.

At the Mirrielees dorm desk and during the quarter I spent studying abroad in Paris, I wrote and wrote for my younger self, the dancer who was so in love with ballet that she gave up all the typical teenage experiences. From the age of twelve, when I went on pointe, until the age of twenty-one, I had thought I knew what I was doing. I had been so sure.

Writing was how I crawled through the years of wishing I'd done it all differently. Eventually, I grew up enough to understand who I was beyond my all-encompassing dancer identity. By then, I'd had a stellar literary agent and heard the rejections from the biggest publishing houses. I heard that ballet was too niche and marketing dance stories was problematic. But the real issue was that I was writing but hadn't learned the craft of fiction. If I wanted to be a writer, I had to train the same way I'd learned how to be a dancer. A little bit every day, for decades.

I was a corporate publishing professional on the Amazon Books team—as far from my ballet career as could be— when Amazon launched its first self-publishing platform, CreateSpace. My husband convinced me to self-publish *Girl in Motion* and the sequel, then titled *Breaking Pointe* (now *Girl on Pointe* because the first title turned into a reality TV show). It had been a decade since I'd written them, and we were pleasantly shocked that over 10,000 copies sold.

Content with what I'd done with those books, I spent the next decade building a family and finding my way back to the studio as a ballet teacher. I kept writing as a blogger for my local indie bookstore and working privately on the craft of fiction. The creative process nurtured the artist within me who couldn't stop dancing.

Fast forward to the pandemic. I wrote *Lauren in the Limelight* when COVID-19 kept most of the world home. It was a story specific to tweens, a group I'd missed with my first two books. The ballet world changed rapidly during that time, and as a Pacific Northwest Ballet School faculty member, I watched it up close, in real-time. We were at the forefront, struggling to do better and prioritize inclusivity and mental health in a way I could have only dreamed about as a ballet student and professional.

Now in my forties, I'm finally close to answering, "Why did I do all that?" I suspect many people find answers mid-life. After two years of querying agents and publishers with *Lauren in the Limelight* and hearing again that ballet was too niche, I published it myself. I founded Rhododendron Press with the knowledge I'd gained from my years in the publishing and ballet industries combined.

In 2023, I completed *Lauren in the Limelight*. At the same time, I revisited the books I'd written in my twenties, seeing their characters anew through my eyes as a mother, an instructor, and a person who cares deeply for the next gen-eration. I continue sharing this art form I love through my studio teaching and solitary writing. I want others to know classical ballet and understand its discipline and immense rewards—it's my way of contributing to the future of ballet and those who will inhabit it. My books were written for the people who bring this art form to life. I want them to find fiction on the shelves to accompany their journeys in the dance world. Whether you're a dancer, a dance lover, or a person who has a dream and follows it, I invite you to find a bit of yourself in my characters' challenges, wonders, and triumphs.

As ever,

Miriam Landis
September 1, 2023

Overture

"Fifteen minutes. Fifteen minutes, please," called the stage manager over the intercom. He interrupted the familiar sound of the orchestra tuning up and the hum of the audience as they settled into their seats.

Dancers checked hair, touched up lipstick, and dusted powder over their faces in the dressing room. The dressers hooked ballerinas into their costumes. Men readjusted their dance belts, and women tucked in the satin ribbons on their pointe shoes.

On stage, two women reviewed choreography together near the red velvet curtain. A shirtless principal in tights jogged in a wide circle around the stage, his body glistening. Near the backdrop, the ballet mistress instructed the principal ballerina, who nodded as she ran her hands over her tutu. The conductor emerged from the shadows to discuss tempo with them. Holding a beer, the artistic director checked out the scene in the opposite wing.

"Ten minutes. Ten minutes, please," called the stage manager.

Ballerinas in costumes gathered around the rosin box to rub their shoes in the sticky powder. The cast for the first ballet on the program started to assemble onstage. A girl fired off jumping jacks to keep warm, another executed karate kicks, and another moved her arms in brisk, wide circles.

"Five minutes. Five minutes, please. This is your five-minute call," called the stage manager.

One girl was in the dressing room downstairs, brushing her damp brown hair into a ponytail. Me. After a minute, I pulled and shaped my hair into a French twist, flat against my scalp.

That was what I did every day. The routine, the people, the excitement, and the beauty were the story of my life.

I bent over to rummage in my theater case, then sat up and caught my blue eyes in the mirror. My gaze burned into my reflection, glowing with intensity. I'd worked hard and been so present. There was no question that I'd earned the right to be there.

Before every show, I reminded myself that my job wasn't about me. My body was there to be an instrument in an orchestra of dancers. Despite the nature of our work, the ballet world *was* personal. How could it not be? I gave everything when I danced for the pleasure of others.

I didn't understand until much later that devoting my life to a professional ballet career meant giving so much.

Every time I performed, I offered up every possible ounce of my time, heart, body, and soul—essentially, a person's most precious gifts.

CHAPTER 1

Mom hailed a taxi, and I told the driver, "JFK airport, please."

We watched the skyscrapers fade as we left the city behind. The moment was bittersweet. I pictured myself in my lavender *Waltz* tutu, a million tiny rhinestones in my hair, bowing my head in a final grand *révérance* to that essential chapter in my life.

I was grateful that high school graduation hadn't been the end. I'd learned so much during my two years at the School of Ballet New York, and after everything I'd been through, I was ready for the next step.

We were on our way to Los Angeles, and it was time for my dance career to begin.

Mom talked to the cab driver on the way to the airport. "We're from Rock Island, Illinois. My daughter here is a ballerina. She's dreamed of a ballet career her entire life and just finished her last two years of high school at SBNY. Sorry, that's the School of Ballet New York, the country's most prestigious ballet school if you didn't know."

I kicked her to make her quiet, but she waved me away. The cabbie gave us a curious look in the rearview mirror.

We were still processing the upheaval of the last few days, and Mom needed to talk about it. "Can I tell you our good news? The Los Angeles Ballet Theater hired her. She was in SBNY's annual Workshop performance, and the artistic director was in the audience. This girl here had a fever but insisted on dancing. She fainted halfway through the ballet. Her alternate had to run onstage and finish her part. The whole thing was wild."

My skin flushed with embarrassment. Did the cabbie need to know all this?

He rubbed his beard and said, "My daughter takes ballet. Well, it's more like creative movement. She's six." He winked at me in the rearview mirror.

Mom brightened like always at the mention of little girls in ballet. Dance made her nostalgic for her childhood. She told him, "If she keeps going, you better be careful. I had no idea what we got ourselves into."

"That's how I felt about potty training," he said.

They laughed, and Mom patted my knee, knowing both that I was mortified and that she couldn't help herself. "We thought her ballet career was over before it started, but the artistic director liked her commitment."

"Why aren't you joining Ballet New York?" asked the cabbie. "Isn't that the big one?"

The question was a punch in the gut. Mom put her hand on my leg because she knew how I'd take it.

"Los Angeles has one of the top five companies in the United States," Mom said, losing her enthusiasm for the conversation.

I stared out the window and thought of the three girls Los Angeles Ballet Theater had hired for the new season. We were all eighteen years old and came from SBNY: Faye Johnson, Hilary Marshall, and me.

We'd dreamed of joining the school-affiliated company, but only one girl from our upper-level class had received a Ballet New York contract after the Workshop. Our small class was already elite, each dancer chosen from the pool of thousands of girls who auditioned worldwide. We were as good if not better than many professional dancers around the country by the time we graduated, so who received a job had more to do with an artistic director's taste and casting needs than with our ability.

My teachers at SBNY had implied that I wasn't the right fit for BNY because I never grew past five foot three, and everyone in the *corps de ballet* of Ballet New York was at least five foot five.

The next day, Mom and I walked from the hotel in Santa Monica to investigate the company studios on the

Third Street Promenade. The giant palm trees were a drastic change from the skyscrapers I was accustomed to in New York. A cool breeze blew in from the ocean, and the air smelled fresh and clean. The sun was supposed to burn off the fog before lunch.

Tourists strolled along the sidewalk. Up ahead, there was a crowd peering into a storefront window, and across the top was a black awning with a banner that pronounced Los Angeles Ballet Theater in elegant cream letters. A home furnishing store was on one side, and a bookstore on the other.

"I can't believe LABT rehearses smack in the middle of a mall," I said.

"Maybe we'll see a celebrity?" Mom asked.

"I'd rather see some LABT dancers," I said. "I'll recognize some of their faces from that program in the SBNY library."

We walked up to the studio windows, which stretched from floor to ceiling. "Wow. There's nowhere to hide," Mom said. Faye wasn't kidding when she'd reported that pedestrians could watch the rehearsals.

I could only imagine what Jen would say if she were here: "Thank goodness the National Ballet Theatre doesn't do that to us." My SBNY roommate's voice would always be in my head. She was back in New York, working on her career at a different company.

Twelve beautiful, athletic women faced the mirror and rehearsed synchronized steps inside the studio. Their pointe shoes clacked against the floor loud enough to hear through the window.

"You look so young compared to them," Mom said, saying my thoughts out loud and attracting attention from bystanders.

I pushed my long hair behind my ears, thinking again of my friends far away, how they confided in me, or how I could share thoughts with them that these professionals would laugh at.

"Is that the ballet mistress?" Mom asked, peering in the window. She tilted her head toward the woman with a notepad at the front of the room, who looked as good as the retired dancers that haunted the Upper West Side in New York. The woman's commanding posture and narrow head gave her a bird-like look. She wore black horn-rimmed glasses and her dark hair in a short ponytail.

My mom was a stark contrast: a plain-faced woman from Illinois who worked in an orthodontist's office. Her hair was as short as Dad's, and she didn't bother with makeup or fashion.

"Probably. Don't point." I recognized the ballet mistress as Lila Jebroy, a former soloist with Ballet San

Francisco. She wore black leggings, a black T-shirt with "Los Angeles Ballet Theater" written in red across the front, and salmon-colored teaching shoes. Lila had a reputation as one of the most demanding bosses in the country. I had heard stories about her even though she was never famous as a dancer. She kicked dancers out of class just for yawning.

Mom put her hand up to the glass. "She looks good. In her fifties, maybe?"

"No idea." I pulled Mom back from the window. It was much easier to go home and enter my parents' world than to have them join mine.

I'd left home to train in New York when I was sixteen and never shared much during our weekly phone calls. Mom would tell me that she ran into so-and-so at the grocery store and found out her daughter had received a National Merit Scholarship. Dad would report back on mowing the lawn and how the college courses he taught were going.

On the other hand, what I wanted to tell them was so removed from their life. Instead of saying, "The new principal dancer in Ballet New York taught our class today, and Hilary messed up right in front of her," I used to say things like, "It's snowing in New York. I should get a new pair of gloves."

After those conversations, my mom wasn't fully prepared to witness my life up close. She was nervous and overly enthusiastic.

"Let's find the staff entrance," I suggested, and she followed me around the building.

Two male dancers in sweatpants and tank tops sat on a bench by the back door. I couldn't remember who they were from the program, but they looked familiar. They were smoking cigarettes and gave me the once-over as I approached.

I asked, "Is this the studio entrance?"

"Who are you?" asked the more diminutive guy. His tone was so matter-of-fact that I couldn't tell if he meant to be nice or rude. His thick brown hair hung like a mop over his eyes, and his posture conveyed a mix of boredom and exhaustion. His chest was much broader than his friend's, and he had a nice-looking, friendly face and the build of a gymnast.

The bigger and meaner-looking guy took a long drag on his cigarette. His reddish hair was cropped short, and his ruddy face seemed older to me, but maybe it was the dark stubble.

"Anna," I said, offering my hand. "I'm one of the new apprentices."

"I'm Susan Forester," Mom said in an eager tone. "Anna's mom. It's *so* nice to meet you both."

"I'm Mikey," said the mop-haired one, shaking my hand.

"Ian," said the redhead after he blew smoke out of the side of his mouth. "When do you start?"

"Monday," I said.

"Then why are you here now?" Ian asked in a mocking tone. He cleared his throat. "You have three more days of freedom."

I could only imagine what he thought of me bringing my mom. "I thought I'd look at the schedule," I said, playing it cool. "You know. Look around."

"She's one of those SBNY bunheads," Ian told Mikey. "They're the same way every year." Ian pointed his foot and examined it. "Don't worry, darling, you'll get over the excitement soon enough."

"Don't let his bitterness infect you," Mikey advised me. He looked at my mom and smiled.

"This is a big change for her," Mom said.

I counted how many minutes I had left until she returned to Rock Island.

We said goodbye, and I pulled the door open. Mom followed me into the front hallway, a threadbare entrance with green linoleum and a company poster on the wall. The air was hot and oppressive.

There was clapping, and the door at the end of the hall flew open. Girls poured out of the studio, trailing snippets of conversation like, "Did you know blueberries are a power food?" and "These pointe shoes are *so* dead." They were covered in sweat, and their leotards stuck to their bodies in patches. The temperature grew warmer from their body heat.

Their colorful outfits were far from the black leotards and pink tights we wore in ballet school. One girl passed me in a floral bathing suit and yoga pants, followed by another wearing a brown halter leotard with zebra legwarmers. How could they look in the mirror and see what their muscles were doing under all those crazy clothes?

"I know your face from SBNY," said a pretty girl with brown hair and dark eyes. I'd been a level behind her in New York and remembered her remarkable extension. She was exactly my height.

Her name was Rebecca, and when I'd known her, she'd been the second in command in the older popular group. She was the one who copied outfits and hairstyles and, despite how pretty she was, always gave off a needy vibe. Her crowd there were the stuck-up and chronically unhappy kids.

"Anna, right? Welcome to the company. Glad you're here." She squeezed my arm before moving on. What a relief that I knew *someone.*

Lila Jebroy came walking down the hall toward my mom and me. She looked right through us. Did she know who I was? Her manner was unapologetic and aggressive.

Mom didn't miss a beat. She stepped right in Lila's path and put out her hand. "I'm Susan Forester, Anna's mother," she said. "We're glad to meet you."

Lila startled, and to my relief, her face relaxed. She introduced herself. "You must be Anne, then," she said, turning to me. "Aren't you a little sprite?"

"Yes, I'm Ann*a*," I said, shaking her hand. Nice to meet you." I wonder if I should call her Lila or Ms. Jebroy.

"Call me Lila," she said, reading my thoughts. "William was pleased you were coming."

"I'm so excited to be here," I said, and my voice sounded hopelessly young.

Lila shoved a pen behind her ear. "We have a lot of ballets to teach you. Rehearsals will be busy next week. I need to run, but feel free to peek in the studios." She looked me over. "I hope you're not out of shape."

"I've only been off a few days," I said.

My mom looked from Lila to me. I tried to smile convincingly.

"Good," Lila pronounced. "See you later." She disappeared down the hall.

"I'm so happy Anna will be a part of this. Thank you," Mom called after her.

Was Lila always like that?

"Well, that was interesting," Mom said.

I followed Lila's direction down the hall and around the corner, hoping to find a rehearsal schedule. Mom trailed behind.

We entered a central lounge connected to all the studios. Dancers crowded the room. I sat Mom down on a bench and begged her to be quiet while I looked at the bulletin board.

A Black girl with high cheekbones stood drinking soda and reading the schedule. She wore a red racer-back leotard with black sweatpants and had one bare foot on the bench. Her toes looked misshapen.

I moved closer to the bench and accidentally brushed a muscular guy with thick eyebrows and dirty blonde hair. A woman in a black unitard with dark hair and skin so pale it was almost translucent sat beside him. I could smell her lilac perfume.

The dancer in the red racer-back leotard said, "Lila wants to put all of *Frontiers* together on Monday."

"I'm not spending what little free time we get studying performance videos," said the one in the black unitard.

The familiar music of the ballet *Violins* floated from behind a closed door. Another rehearsal was in progress. I had been around dancers since I was little, and this world felt like home.

"Are you one of the new apprentices starting next week?" the first girl asked me. "I'm Kelly." She took a long drink from her soda can and pointed at the other two dancers. "That's Elizabeth and Ryan. You should go to all these complete rehearsals." She tilted her head toward the schedule. "Lila taught everyone's parts in *Frontiers* during the last two weeks, and Monday will be the first time we run the whole ballet with everyone together. That rehearsal on Monday afternoon is probably to catch you up."

"Have I missed a lot?" I asked.

"You'll see *Frontiers* every day this summer. In two weeks, you'll know it backward. It would be best if you came to *Georgia on my Mind* too," Kelly added, bending her right leg at the knee, grabbing the arch of her foot, and pulling it toward her back to stretch her quad. "Someone will get injured."

"You better not mean me," said Elizabeth, standing and stretching her arms over her head. Her body in the black unitard was one long, thin line, primarily legs.

Ryan stood up. "No one is getting injured," he said, flipping back his unkempt hair. When he smiled, I noticed his bright blue eyes. He was handsome and confident: dangerous qualities in a straight ballet guy.

I told myself right then and there not to develop a crush. Most of the other girls in the company probably liked him. He was that kind of guy, and there were never enough of them to go around in ballet.

Ryan glanced at the clock on the wall. "Duty calls," he said.

Elizabeth shouldered her bag and went into the nearest studio, leaving the scent of lilac perfume behind her. Ryan followed her. His back muscles rippled under his T-shirt as he walked away.

At least there was at least one straight guy in the company, *and* he was cute.

"Where are you living?" Kelly asked.

"Downtown, just south of the Pier, on Main Street," I said. "We wanted something within walking distance. I'm rooming with one of the other new apprentices."

"That quiet girl from Queens?" Kelly asked, bending backward until her spine cracked. "I met her Wednesday. Faye, right? Or do you mean the rude redhead?"

It was hard not to laugh at Kelly's description of Hilary, my former SBNY roommate. I didn't want to think about her. "Yes, I'm rooming with Faye," I said. In New York, Faye lived at home instead of in the dorms, so we never hung out outside class. Kelly was right that Faye was shy and hard to read, but I'd take her any day over Hilary.

I told Kelly about the one-year lease that we'd signed on a furnished two-bedroom, one-bathroom apartment. Having someone else's furniture was strange. At least the building was close to the studios and had big windows that let in plenty of sunlight. It wasn't worth committing to furniture or anything else permanent until we knew if our jobs would work out.

While we talked, I looked closer at the schedule. "Is it true we dance eight hours a day? Is there a lunch break?"

"About eight hours. Lunch is at two," Kelly said, pointing at the schedule to show me. "They rehearse the principals during our break."

In ballet school, I had a vague idea of what company life would be like. Now that I was about to start a real job, wearing pointe shoes for eight hours a day seemed unbearable. At SBNY, I only had to wear them for about four to six. It had been years since I'd danced in soft ballet slippers because SBNY expected the upper-level girls to wear pointe shoes in every class.

"If my feet hurt too much, will Lila understand if I need to dance in ballet slippers?" I asked.

Kelly laughed, and I knew what that meant. Everyone would think I was weak or lazy. Taking my pointe shoes off wasn't going to be a realistic option.

"You'll get used to it," she said. "Everyone knows it's different to dance a ballet on pointe than in technique shoes. You went to SBNY. They taught us to rehearse the same way we perform. I got through it. You can, too." She looked amused as she picked up her bag and said she had to get to rehearsal.

I watched her walk down the hall. She was at least two inches taller than me.

My mom walked up next to me. "I peeked in on a rehearsal," she confessed. "I have no idea how anyone can do this."

"Practice," I said. "Can we get some lunch?"

I was exhausted by all the new information. The dancers who made it to SBNY had been unusually gifted, but the professionals were the cherry-pickings of an already elite group.

The stakes were even higher in a company. Ballet wasn't a hobby or a passion anymore.

From here on out, this was my career.

CHAPTER 2

On the first day of work, Faye and I arrived at the studio half an hour before class. We'd already been up for hours, doing our hair and makeup and studying the headshots and bios in an old LABT program. The building was deserted.

"Don't professionals warm up?" I asked.

"Apparently not," Faye said, following me into the women's dressing room.

By the time we'd changed our clothes, dancers crowded the locker room and stood around in various stages of undress. Kelly shot me a friendly smile. On that first day, my blue leotard, pink tights, purple leg warmers, and black skirt screamed "student" next to what everyone else put on.

"How dare Lila try to tone down my style?" Natasha Fedorova said to another principal, Adrienne Castle, one of LABT's most famous dancers. Natasha pulled on a leopard print unitard and said that Lila had told her the outfit was blinding people.

Adrienne had been on the cover of *Dance Magazine* a few months earlier. She had a girl-next-door quality. It was like looking at someone and knowing you'd want them as a friend.

"Everyone knows you have a big personality," Adrienne told Natasha. They laughed, and several dancers chimed in with words of support.

The culture in the dressing room was a significant part of company life. It took time to understand that apart from the occasional conversations about injuries or after-work plans, we did little in there except commiserate, change clothes, or collapse from exhaustion. Something about the atmosphere inspired relaxation we could never show in the studio.

A blonde with pencil-thin legs watched Faye open a locker. "Those are for the principals," she said. Her face looked like she'd done some hard living.

Faye turned pink and apologized. She moved away to a different corner. I felt so embarrassed for her.

The blonde didn't care. She heaved a floral bag exploding with pointe shoes over her shoulder and tossed a pair of tights into the trash. "Those had one too many holes," she grumbled, letting the door slam as she left the dressing room.

I tied my skirt and squeezed past Kelly and Elizabeth, the two dancers I'd met earlier, to check my reflection.

"How's your knee?" Kelly asked Elizabeth.

Elizabeth pulled up black tights over her brown leotard and said, "Better, thanks. The swelling went down. I should be fine for *Frontiers*." The smell of lavender body splash wafted toward me as Elizabeth sprayed it across her neck and chest.

"Are you going to see Carla?" Kelly asked.

Elizabeth made a scared face and said, "It'll go away on its own. Lila and William will hear if I see Carla for physical therapy."

When I walked into the studio behind Faye, there was Hilary, already at a front-of-the-room spot at a portable barre.

I resolved to give her another chance. She was sitting with her hips in the frog position, the bottoms of her feet touching and her knees on the ground. Her leotard was new, a fancy green velvet with a low back and gold trim. We gave each other a small wave.

Faye crossed the room to a spot near the window.

Kelly was stretching next to a portable barre near the wall. I caught her eye. "Is there a good place for me to stand?" I inched closer to her. "I don't want to take anyone's spot."

"You mean like her?" Kelly gave a dramatic roll of her eye toward Hilary. "Elizabeth is not going to like her standing there. Come behind me, here," she said. "Adam usually stands there, but he has a back injury." She pushed deeper into a perfect middle split and glanced at her reflection.

"Who's Adam?" I put my bag down.

Still watching herself in the mirror, she said, "This is probably his last season. After he turned forty, William took him out of some of his regular roles."

In the morning light, the studio felt like a sanctuary where people came to worship. If I ever had a moment of doubt, it was then, as I put on my pointe shoes and tried to understand what Kelly meant. Who *was* William Mason? How much did I want to be here? Could I trust anyone?

Pedestrians stared through the window from the Third Street Promenade.

"It's a brilliant business tactic, right?" Kelly said. "You'd think those people had never seen a girl in a leotard and tights before."

"Isn't that storefront a recipe for stalkers?" I asked.

"I'm not going to lie, it's happened," Kelly said. "But most people who look at what we do are genuinely curious. It's good for public relations."

I sat down, stretched over my extended legs, and grabbed my ankles. With a deep breath, I buried my nose in my knees. My body felt stiff. Lila had been right. It had been over a week since I last took class, and I had to coax my muscles into cooperation.

Hilary approached and asked how I'd been, and Kelly gave her a suspicious look. Kelly was a sharp one.

"Did you know William teaches company class every day?" Hilary whispered.

"Are you nervous?" I asked.

"Of course not," she said. "I thought you'd appreciate the advance notice."

I asked her about her apartment and told her where Faye and I had moved. She said she was glad to have her own space. That brought up bad memories of fighting with her when we were roommates. I didn't want to think about our history together.

Hilary headed back to her barre, but Elizabeth had taken her spot while she'd been talking to me.

"I usually stand here," Elizabeth said with a glare.

"Can I stand behind you?" Hilary asked.

"This barre is always full," Elizabeth said. "You can stand over there." She pointed to a spot way in the corner.

Hilary chewed on her lip. "In the back?"

"Yep, in the back," Elizabeth said.

Elizabeth turned away. Hilary picked up her bag and headed to the other spot. She wasn't used to anyone talking to her that way. I almost felt sorry for her. Almost.

I placed my hand on the barre and stood with my heels touching. My toes pointed flat to each side at a hundred-and-eighty-degree angle. Out of the corner of my eye, I checked myself in the mirror and pulled up every muscle I could while pushing my shoulders toward the ground and lengthening my neck. To test out my latest pair of shoes, I slowly rolled up onto pointe and down to a deep *plié*, my knees bending while my heels remained on the floor.

Mikey took the spot across from me at the portable barre. His hair was a mess. "Ten o'clock. Ugh," Mikey said. He sat there and sipped his coffee, too tired to warm up.

The room filled up. The company members greeted each other and filled the room with purpose.

At ten o'clock on the dot, William walked into the studio. I remembered the last time I'd seen him, alone in Madame Sivenko's office in New York. He was the most charismatic man I'd ever seen, and when he fixed his eyes on me and offered me a contract, he'd instantly turned me into someone special.

This William was different in the context of forty-five of his hand-picked dancers. I wasn't the focus of his attention here—he was the special one. He looked invigorated and much younger than sixty, dressed in a T-shirt, khaki trousers, and jazz shoes. His broad shoulders looked strong enough to throw a 70-yard touchdown.

The elderly Russian pianist opened the piano lid. "That's Olga," Mikey whispered. "She's been with William for ages."

Instead of demonstrating a *plié* combination as I expected, William gestured to Olga. With a great flourish, Olga began a slow and steady 4/4 march. The company knew what to do. I put my left hand on the barre and followed Kelly, wondering how many years some of these dancers had taken his class.

William walked around the room as we danced, quietly observing. Everyone tried harder as he passed by.

At the end of the third combination, William held up his hand. "I forgot," he announced. "Let's welcome our new apprentices, Faye, Hilary, and Anna." The room exploded in a mix of applause, whistles, and catcalls. Faye and I exchanged embarrassed looks.

A tall principal I recognized as Lorenzo Diaz came and shook my hand. "Great to have you," he said, and I remembered Kelly mentioning that Lorenzo was Elizabeth's boyfriend.

When the noise calmed down, the class continued. William clapped out the rhythm and counted along with the music. "And one. And two. Three and four. Five and six and seven and eight. And one. And two. Three and four. Five and six and seven and eight."

The way that William syncopated the music was new. He focused on what was happening in our heads rather than how we looked. At SBNY, they always corrected us on how we held our arms or presented our feet. In William's class, the focus seemed to be our thought process and how we moved to the music.

Forty minutes later, we came off the barres to the center. Faye and I huddled together in the back corner as dancers took their places around the room. We compared notes and agreed we couldn't understand the musicality.

I tried the *adagio* and ended up dancing squished against the back wall. There were too many people around to find space. The *pirouette* combination was no better. How would I get used to this?

William indicated a small jump. The dancers executed the step, traveling forward from the back in groups of eight.

I stared at Adrienne, the *Dance Magazine* cover girl. Every muscle was perfectly defined, and her body looked like music when she moved.

Natasha's dancing was much more classical than the other principals'. She held her upper body beautifully, but Adrienne and Elizabeth moved much faster, with more energy in their legs.

Jeff Abbott, another principal, criticized Ian for getting in his way. "Are you always this stupid, or are you making a special effort today?" Jeff said.

"Maybe if you stopped staring at yourself in the mirror, you'd notice the traffic," Ian shot back.

Someone behind me touched my shoulder and said, "It takes time to get used to everything." Startled, I turned and looked up into William's reassuring face. I'd been so focused on Adrienne that I hadn't noticed he'd walked up behind me.

Looking into his eyes, I understood something. When William chose me out of all the hiring options he'd seen in New York, he'd looked at the candidates through the lens of someone who spent his day-to-day life training Adrienne Castle and the other dancers in the room. I'd compared myself to the other students at SBNY. He had judged me by the world of this company.

William moved past me to talk with Natasha. She laughed out loud after he whispered something in her ear.

The class was so different than any previous training. It wasn't just the proficiency of the dancers. What changed was the feeling that we all danced for the sake of one person: him. Even the principals must have had William in mind when they danced. He was the reason every one of us was there.

"That's the end, Olga," William said, raising his hand to the pianist. "Thanks, guys." The room broke out in scattered applause as everyone dispersed. I sat down, took a long swig from my water bottle, and noticed Adrienne kissing Zif Sumanga.

"They've been married since high school," Kelly said, noticing my stare.

"Anna Forester," a voice called in a loud stage whisper. A short, older Chinese man was in the doorway, gesturing at me. Hilary and Faye were already standing beside him. I hurried over.

"Tong here," he said, giving me a little bow. "I run the wardrobe and shoe department. Come with me. We'll get you the perfect pointe shoes. You'll look fabulous."

Faye, Hilary, and I exchanged a look of glee and followed him down the hall. Free shoes! We had waited our entire lives for this.

"Finally. Custom-made shoes," Faye whispered, squeezing my hand.

"I never thought this day would come," I whispered. Even Hilary couldn't help smiling.

"I'm easy to find when you need me," said Tong, chattering a mile a minute as we walked. "If you see a needle and thread or a spectacular hairdo, I've been there. I love my dancers. I just love them."

He ushered us into the spacious wardrobe and shoe room, filled with treasures. There were elaborate tutus and rows of leotards and jewel-adorned tunics. One wall had floor-to-ceiling cubbies of pointe shoes divided by last names. I fingered a sparkly bodice and imagined wearing it.

Tong pulled out his tape and documented every possible measurement. He wrote down our shoe specifications, too.

"Perfection," he muttered as he measured the circumference of my head. "Look at that long neck, and that face!"

He went on about his work, offering us compliments and promising to rush order our shoes. "You'll have to wear stock shoes until your custom pairs arrive, and here are your theater cases. You'll need these for tours and when we perform. I'm sorry, but I only have two new trunks, so someone gets a used one. You can write your names on them." He pulled out three black cases that looked like they came off a Broadway show truck.

Hilary grabbed a new trunk, and after I said I'd take the used case, Faye took the other.

"Welcome to the company," Tong said. "Now, shoo. Go to rehearsal."

I stopped in the break room and grabbed some caffeine before returning to the studio. As Faye and I rounded a corner, I ran smack into Jeff Abbott, spilling my coffee all down the front of his shirt.

Pulling the cloth away from his torso, he shouted, "That's *hot*."

My face flushed. While I apologized, he muttered obscenities and tried to clean himself up.

"This would be a good time for you to become a missing person, new girl," Jeff snapped at me.

"It was an accident," I said helplessly. He ignored me.

I turned and fled down the hall.

Rehearsals. There wasn't much space to practice in the back of the room. I was the second cast for everything. When the first cast finished their run-through, they put Faye, Hilary, and me in with the other dancers for the first time.

We didn't know what to do or where to go and nearly knocked people over. I barely understood the steps or the spacing, even though Lila had reviewed everything with us before. There wouldn't be a mirror onstage, and I could only get through the choreography by checking other dancers in the reflection.

"You'll need to develop a sixth sense," Kelly told me.

"Or a third eye in the back of my head," I said.

A minute later, I saw Jeff talking to Natasha and Allison across the room. He gestured in my direction, obviously telling them the coffee story. Allison glanced over at me and squeezed his arm sympathetically.

"Don't worry about Jeff," Kelly whispered, having heard what happened. "He's a grouch. That's why he and Mikey break up every other month." The accident hung over my head like a dark cloud.

Jeff complaining about me to Natasha and Allison was bad news. Both had political power within the company. People would listen if they had an unfavorable opinion of me.

By the second Friday of work, my body hurt almost as much as my self-esteem. Thank goodness I didn't have to return to the studio for two days. It was a miracle that my feet hadn't fallen off. Even after years of pointe classes, eight hours a day in pointe shoes was much more than I could tolerate. And there was so much choreography to remember. My brain was ready to implode.

We were in the dressing room at the end of the day, and I could hardly move. "Let's go home," Faye urged me for the third time. She looked equally exhausted.

Pulling myself off the bench, I followed Faye out of the building. The late-day sun felt good on my shoulders. We waved at Mikey and Ian, who were smoking on the bench.

"Have a good weekend," I said, but there was too much of a social scene in progress for anyone to notice. Rebecca was chatting with Ryan, her hand resting possessively on his knee. Lorenzo told a skeptical-looking Jeff how he and Ryan charmed the female donors at a benefit. Allison looked even moodier than usual, shooting an annoyed glare at Ian, who complained to Mikey about hurting his foot in rehearsal.

Faye and I passed them and headed home. People turned and looked at us, walking down the Third Street Promenade with our pinned-up hair, turned-out walk, and net bags filled with pointe shoes.

"Forester. Sheridan. Wait up," Mikey called behind us. We stopped and waited for him. "Are you coming to my party tomorrow? It's BYOB. Oh, wait. You aren't old enough."

"Thanks for the reminder," Faye said.

"We might not make it. We have a lot of ballet videos to watch," I said, only half-kidding.

Mikey rolled his eyes. Before disappearing into the crowd, he looked over his shoulder and said, "Be there. I'll text you with the address."

It was not a request. Company expectations extended beyond the studio.

That night, after Faye and I spent the evening studying a video of *Frontiers,* I left her making tea in the kitchen and went into the bedroom to call my parents. Because of the time difference, it was late enough that my dad was home from work and picked up the phone.

"Dad," I said, happy to hear his voice. "I miss you." My obsession with ballet had always mystified him.

"I miss you too," he said. "Although, admit it, if you were home, you'd be bored a minute after you saw the cat."

"I'm homesick."

Mom came on the line. "Why the sad voice?" she said. "You're in one of the best ballet companies in the country. When I was your age, I would have killed for a life like yours. Living in LA in my own apartment, surrounded by beautiful people, fulfilling my dream . . ."

I flopped back on the bed.

"I know what you need," Dad said. "A car. You'll want it in the fall when you go to the theater, or the company performs in Palm Springs and San Diego."

"How am I old enough to have a health plan, a retirement fund, and a car?" I asked. "Rachel is starting Northwestern, and Marie will be at Columbia in the fall. How am I on such a different planet?"

"In four years, the kids in college now will be doing the same thing you are," said Mom. "Everyone starts a career eventually; you just started sooner."

"You can always change your mind and get your degree instead," Dad said lightly.

They weren't wrong, but their practicality didn't make my feelings easier. "I'll be fine, don't worry about me. I'm just having a bad night, is all."

Before we hung up, Dad said, "It's not you I'm worried about. It's that world."

Faye had the *Frontiers* video on again in the living room. I couldn't bear to go out there and watch it again.

My side of the room was a mess, so I started cleaning. After I folded and put away my laundry, I opened the theater case and piled my pointe shoes and extra warm-ups inside. There was a stray pair of shoes under the bed, and I pulled them out and tossed them across the room into the open case. One shoe hit the lid. The inside dropped, exposing a hidden compartment.

I sat down in front of the case and performed a closer examination. The lid had a false cover. The hidden space was empty, except for one pink silk pocket on the upper left side. I reached inside and pulled out what looked like a journal.

The dramatic music from *Frontiers* seeped through the door and heightened the moment. It crossed my mind to call Faye and show her what I found, but I hesitated, and the moment passed.

The book was probably nothing, but maybe I'd found a secret.

My fingers traced the embossed gold design on the cover before I flipped it open. The journal was handwritten and dense, page after page filled with scribbled writing in blue pen. I flipped through it, looking for a name. There wasn't one, so I turned to the beginning and started to read.

How could this happen to me? I broke my leg rehearsing the third movement of Fire. *Lila kept pushing me to jump more and lift my leg higher (it was a jump where I kicked my left leg out to the side and pushed off the right standing leg). I was trying so hard to do the step how she wanted, and then I didn't even know what happened, but I landed at the wrong angle, and my leg slipped, and I fell hard on my left side. Everyone heard the snap. I screamed so loud. My leg was sticking out at a strange angle. They called an ambulance. The rest was a blur. I'm scared I might never be able to dance again.*

I stopped. Was she a recent company member? Her accident sounded like my worst nightmare. The broken leg might have ended her career. An injury like that is where I drew a blank. I couldn't even imagine what came next.

How did the diary end up in my theater case? I'd have to ask around and see who the journal belonged to.

CHAPTER 3

Faye and I spent an hour getting ready before Mikey's party. We made ourselves up and put on bright tank tops and skirts. Once we got out the door, I changed my mind and ran back to switch to jeans and a T-shirt. Faye stuck to the original plan and waited patiently. "I felt like I was trying too hard," I explained.

I barely recognized Ian when he greeted us in a blonde wig, pink dress, stilettos, and a feather boa at the door. He had shaved the dark stubble on his chin, stuffed a bra, lined his eyes with black liner, and applied heavy false eyelashes.

Ian made a beautiful woman. "My goldfish died today," he lamented, pressing the back of his hand to his forehead. "Come, mourn with me over a drink. Welcome to Mikey's apartment. I live in the same building, so this is practically my other home."

"Have you ever seen a man in drag?" Faye whispered as we followed Ian down the hall.

"Not in real life," I said.

We followed Ian past a cluster of people in the living room. He swung his hips and held his arms daintily in front of his chest like paws. I wasn't sure how he wanted us to react. Ian was a *corps de ballet* member in the ballet studio, but here, as the only drag queen at the party, he commanded everyone's attention.

The kitchen counter was set up as a full-service bar. Ian fixed both of us a vodka and cranberry. "Lorenzo is here," Ian whispered. "Just for the record, I'm in love with him and waiting for him to dump Elizabeth."

Ian had good taste. Lorenzo was gorgeous, and he'd been friendly and shook my hand on my first day. Ian could have said the same thing about any of the principals, and I would have understood. The higher someone's rank and the better their dance ability, the more desirable they were.

"I suspect Lorenzo has a waiting list," Faye said.

"Mikey and Jeff are a thing again, and I'm bored," Ian said. He fluffed Faye's brown hair. "Honey, we should get you some highlights."

She flushed. "I've never colored my hair before. Are you and Mikey a thing?"

Ian laughed and said, "God, no. We're good friends. Back to your hair. An apprentice should have some fun before thirty-five performances of *Nutcracker*. You'll never get the music out of your head. Every store you enter plays the Sugar

Plum Fairy variation on a loop. Dink dink dink, dink dink, dink, dink-dink-dink . . . There are a hundred screaming kids with their mothers lurking around backstage. In the party scene, all we do is stand there. There's no dancing. The guys wear those putrid mouse costumes twice a day. The audience isn't the regular crowd because they know better. Families come as their holiday tradition, which is why *Nutcracker* is a cash cow and will never go away."

"You have to admit there are good parts, like when the tree grows and snow falls onstage," I said. "It also means we get to be in every single show." The apprentices danced every performance as Snow, Spanish, Waltz of the Flowers, and sometimes Marzipan if we were lucky.

"We'll talk after the twentieth performance," Ian said. "Then you tell me how magical *Nuts* is."

At that point, I surveyed the scene. I'd never been comfortable at parties and preferred a small group of close friends.

Rebecca, the girl I knew from SBNY, was leaning against a wall nearby, talking to a few other *corps de ballet* girls about the indie music scene. She looked stunning in wedge sandals and a funky dress resembling a pink lava lamp. "Let's get together and camp at that music festival next time we're on layoff," I heard her tell the others. "We can rally those cute guys from the bike shop."

To my surprise, she gestured at me to come over. Suddenly, I wished I hadn't changed out of the fancier outfit.

She clinked plastic cups with me. "How are you?"

"Thanks again for going over the counts for *Fire* with me," I said. There were only eight *corps de ballet* spots in *Fire*, and twenty-two girls in the lower ranks at LABT. It was a big deal they'd cast me in it.

Rebecca said, "*Fire* is tricky to count. The Stravinsky ballets are a challenge. That's quite a compliment that Lila put you in the second cast."

"Didn't Hilary dance the *Fire* lead in the SBNY Workshop?" asked the dancer standing next to Rebecca. "I heard Stacy Hannah staged it."

I flashed back to my last experience with *Fire*. Eight months earlier, the teachers at SBNY cast Hilary, another girl, and me as the leads. We were supposed to share the role and each dance one performance. I was so excited. Fire was my favorite ballet, and the boy I liked, Tyler, was my partner. The original dancer—Stacy Hannah—whom Roizman choreographed the ballet for, taught us the role.

After months of rehearsal, the school changed its mind and took me out of the ballet. They said I was too short to get into Ballet New York. I was devastated. Later, I heard that Hilary's parents had made a massive donation to the school on the condition that she dance multiple performances of the role.

There was no justice when it came to casting.

I said, "Do either of you know of a girl in the company who broke her leg?"

Rebecca exchanged a look with the dancer next to her. "You mean Karina Huntington, who left about five years ago? That's the one I know of."

The other one said, "Karina was out for a year and tried to return, but she left a few months after they put her back onstage. It was a weird situation."

I was more intrigued than ever. The author was real.

Someone turned the music up. The noise from the party drifted out into the street.

CHAPTER 4

I've been injured for a few months now. Every day, I go to physical therapy, and sometimes I watch class or rehearsals, but sometimes I can't take it. There's so much empty time. I'm on worker's compensation. They say my job will be there when I return, but I don't know if I believe them.

Every week that passes, I lose ground. Other dancers are coming up and taking my parts. I would go home to see my mom in Minnesota, but I can't handle the cold weather. My therapy is here anyway. I haven't heard from my dad in years, and sometimes I wonder about tracking him down. I don't think he'd want to hear from me now. There's a reason he left when I was five.

I can't imagine leaving the company. This is my home. It'll work out if I stay focused.

I've always wanted to write, and now I have this recovery time. I asked William about starting a book of interviews. He didn't take my idea seriously but felt sorry for me. He agreed to a brief chat about his role in the company. Here's what he said:

William: *"My run at LABT has been very controversial, and I'd be the first to say that I fail regularly. And, you know, sometimes I want to give up. But it continues to be a meaningful experience. Great experience. You see, I learn a lot every day. I do. It isn't easy because I want to create a dynamic company that can do different styles and perform classical ballets on a higher level. I'm one of the few remaining Roizman dancers who can uphold the tradition, and I take great pride in that. But we need to keep moving forward, too.*

When I first took over LABT, it was unusual to have modern choreographers doing pieces for classical companies. Then people asked, what the hell is he doing? What's next? Nowadays, that kind of new work is expected, but when I started, everyone, from the folks on the street to the critics, thought I was crazy. I knew what I was doing; it was time for new ideas in the theater, and many more unknown choreographers had fresh points of view on classical companies.

I wanted to choreograph, too. I did that the first few years, but my pieces never had the intended impact. The other chore-ographers I brought in were people I used to work with. We're a different generation. The company looks at me like they'd like to get some of this older man's ideas. They're looking to understand the complexity of aging because they don't have many opportunities to work with "old" people. So, I like to bring in older retired dancers with life experience to make new ballets. It's a different vocabulary and accumulation of experiences that young people don't have.

I knew LABT needed a school. We had no breeding ground for younger dancers, and I had no choice but to hire away from other programs. As an institution, we will only be of the highest caliber once we train our dancers. So, we got that started a few years after I lost interest in choreographing. Some things I succeed at. Some I fail. Either way, I must keep trying, keep persisting. That's how this company has become what it is today.

Working with dancers is a delicate and challenging thing. They are emotional creatures, and they started as young children. All they know is dance, and ballet is their whole world. They take it very seriously, as I do. I want them to succeed; I do. But not everyone can. This is a tough life. Survival of the fittest and all that, you know.

I'm very close with the dancers. I love and admire them. I do. I can't dance anymore, so I dance through them. We have the most beautiful dancers in the world. People come to see us to marvel at the beauty of our ballerinas. I'm very proud of them."

Karina's diary lingered in my thoughts. I couldn't read too much at once because it made my head spin. Entering her world took me back in time, and then, every morning, I had to go in and work with many of the same people she wrote about. I knew things about them they didn't know I knew. Her journal was the best secret I'd ever had.

Almost every night after work, I sewed ribbons and elastic onto a new pair of pointe shoes. Pointe shoes only came as a simple slip-on, so I had a whole routine with each new pair before I felt comfortable wearing them to class or rehearsal.

Once I attached the elastic and ribbons so they would wrap around my ankles, I cut the satin off the toe to prevent slipping. Bending the shank made the bottom of the shoe flexible enough to show off my arches when I went up on pointe. I gently closed the door's crack on the toe box so my shoes were quiet when I jumped.

The pointe shoes died faster than they ever did at ballet school. Money was tight for company operations, so as generous as Tong was, we still received a limited supply. I could have gone through more than LABT's three allotted pairs a week if the company had been able to afford it. Their life span depended on the ballets I danced. Sometimes, soft, broken-in shoes were more comfortable for rehearsal. But dancing ballets with a lot of pointe work in dead shoes felt like jamming my toes into the sharp tip of a knife.

Faye and I went to the beach or the movies during our few hours off work, and Dad helped me buy a used sedan when he visited.

"Don't be scared. Just press on the gas," Dad commanded when we bought the car. "It's like living. You do it and let whatever will happen happen."

When Faye and I didn't walk home together because of different schedules, I liked to walk the long way through the residential neighborhoods. The beautiful homes and tree-lined streets made me think about family. Domestic life seemed so far away.

I stopped on one of my favorite blocks to get my sunglasses out of my bag. Suddenly, there was crushing pain in my head, and I fell sideways to the ground, hitting the sidewalk. My pointe shoes flew onto the grass, and momentarily, I lost consciousness.

There was a thump as someone jumped out of a tree.

"Are you OK?" a male voice asked.

I opened my eyes and saw a guy studying me. He looked about my age. From the first moment I laid eyes on him, he felt like a threat to my ballet world. He had a giant electric saw in one hand. Despite the pain in my head, my heart beat a little faster.

"What happened?" I asked, dizzy. "And why are you brandishing that at me?" I touched my head gingerly. "Ow."

"I was pruning the tree," he said, "and I didn't see you below. A branch fell on your head. Should I call an ambulance?"

"How did you not see me?" I asked, disliking him immediately. "Who chainsaws a branch and doesn't make sure the coast is clear?"

"Let me—" he started, but I cut him off.

"Don't you dare call 911. I'm fine." I felt a growing apprehension. No way did I need his help.

"Let me at least get an ice pack for your head." He jogged into the house. I tried to get my bearings. When I touched my head, I felt a lump forming. My hair was still pinned up from work, and I took out the clip, letting it fall around my shoulders.

He couldn't have been more than a few years older than me. That must be his parents' house, I thought. The Mediterranean-style home had a front patio and a meticulously landscaped front yard. I wondered what it was like inside.

He reappeared with a bag of ice. "Do you want to sit on the porch? Is it hard to move?" When I didn't respond, he walked over to help me up.

"I've got it," I said, but my vision blurred. He watched, and when I couldn't mobilize, he helped me to my feet, placing the ice pack on my head and moving my hand to hold the ice.

"Don't laugh," I said. "That's rude."

The pain in my head was intense.

"What's your name?" he asked. "Do you need me to call someone for you? Are you on your way somewhere? I'm Ethan."

I told him my name and that I was on my way home from work. At the same time, I realized I had no one to call in an emergency. Faye wouldn't know what to do except contact my parents.

He picked up my scattered pointe shoes and guided me to a porch chair. There was dirt from the garden all over his clothes and face.

"I'll just sit for a minute," I said, frustrated. My head throbbed.

He sat down next to me, kicked off his shoes, and put his legs up casually on the rail. "Are you in high school? You look like a ballet student. If so, I'm in serious trouble."

He had some nerve to joke after he'd almost killed me. "I'm a professional ballerina, thank you very much."

He flinched. After a moment, he said, "Well, la-dee-da."

"What do you know about it?" I said. "And I'm eighteen, not that it's your business."

"I've seen the ballet a few times," he said. "Have you ever seen the Los Angeles Ballet Theater? My mom was on the board and did early fundraising when the company got off the ground. I always liked watching the pretty girls in the window."

"Yuck," I said, standing up. My head was starting to clear. "For your information, I'm *in* the Los Angeles Ballet Theater."

"I didn't mean to offend you," he said. He looked me in the eye and waited, and I thought, Oh no, this is trouble; what if this guy shows up at my work and waves at me?

The front door opened, and an attractive young woman with long blonde hair came out on the porch.

"Who is this?" she asked Ethan, tilting her head toward me as if I wasn't there.

"I'm just going," I said, leaving the explanation to him.

On the morning we left for our first tour of the season, George, our company manager, passed out the airplane tickets at the studio. He was a former dancer, and always looked frazzled. The trip involved so many logistics.

The company gathered in the parking lot at work, and a bus drove us all to the airport together. I already loved the experience of going on the road: packing my makeup in my theater case, picking out pointe shoes for performances, and watching the company members arrive with their bags packed.

The airport was crowded, and our group made the security line painfully long. George breathed a sigh of relief as we gathered at the gate, headed for Charlotte, North Carolina.

When we boarded the plane, the pilot announced us over the intercom. "It's our great pleasure to be the preferred airlines of William Mason and the Los Angeles Ballet Theater dancers. We want to extend a special welcome to them on this flight."

The older dancers hardly noticed the announcement, but Faye and I grinned at each other. I caught Hilary smiling, too, as she took her seat, despite how cool she tried to appear on the bus. She wore a short skirt, heels, and oversize sunglasses. Most of us were in company-logo sweats.

William and Lila settled into their seats in first class as the rest of us filed into coach. The couples, Rebecca and Ryan, Elizabeth and Lorenzo, and Adrienne and Zif, cuddled up and sat together. Kelly and the other single *corps* girls had their gossip magazines out. Allison and Natasha, who had non-dancer partners at home, sat together and complained about the schedule. Mikey, Ian, Jeff, and the other gay boys huddled around a Nintendo Switch. I found my aisle seat next to Faye and took out Karina's diary.

"What are you reading?" Faye asked, putting away her knitting needles.

"Just an old journal," I said. She gave me a funny look, shrugged, and put on her headphones.

Yesterday, I interviewed Lorenzo for my book project. We've been partners in several ballets, and he's so great. All the girls, and probably the boys, have a crush on him. I'd drop the dentist I've been seeing and go out with him if he showed any romantic interest.

Lorenzo: *"We must have talent, but at the end of the day, that only accounts for some of our success. Eighty percent is hard work. Ballet demands determination and an uncompromising work ethic. I get a lot of satisfaction out of pushing that hard and feeling my body collapse at the end of the day. That's a powerful feeling. We all think we're superhuman until something terrible happens, like what happened to you, Karina. That was so scary.*

I came from a small, poverty-stricken town in Mexico. My parents owned a restaurant. Growing up, I had no exposure to the arts. Ballet came to me as a surprise. All I knew was the poor people's lives in our village, and there were many drug addicts. My younger brother was chronically ill, and we had no money to take him to the hospital or buy medicine. I had to find a way to get him the care he needed.

The day my life changed was in the middle of summer. I was playing basketball with some buddies and wearing my dad's shorts, which were too big for me. These American men pulled up in a car and stopped to watch. They told us they were starting a dance school in Mexico City and wanted to recruit boys for the program. The tallest man said I had talent. Within a week, I went to live in Mexico City to study ballet on full scholarship.

My parents were thrilled I was getting out of there, and so was I. I didn't even know what ballet was, but I loved it immediately and knew I was good at it. I worked in the office at the ballet school and made money to send back to my family. We were able to find out that my younger brother had diabetes and get him the treatment he needed. Ballet changed my life and saved him.

You asked where I see myself in twenty years, and I struggle with that question. I want to get married and have a family, but it's hard to imagine now. My primary relationship is with dance. I can't imagine dating a non-dancer because the girls in dance understand me so well. Most ballerinas are not ready to have babies, at least not at this point in their lives. I would like to see my family in Mexico more, and I imagine I will teach or do something else in ballet when I retire. That's a long way away, though. I'm only twenty-six and probably have another ten years if I'm lucky.

It's hard to say how I feel about William. All the girls worship him, and of course, I admire him. He had a fantastic career. I think he wishes he was still dancing, and he bristles if I show interest in a woman in the company. We get along best when I stay focused on my work.

On opening night in Charlotte, we had class onstage, followed by the dress rehearsal. Before signing in for the half-hour call, there was barely enough time to eat a quick snack.

The girls' dressing room buzzed with activity as I pinned up my hair and applied makeup. Makeup, hairpins, tights, and pointe shoes exploded all over the room. I observed how the experienced *corps* dancers prepared.

"Does my makeup look OK?" I asked Kelly.

She inspected me. "I'd add more blush and darken the eyeliner," she said. "Let me help you."

I was only in the last ballet, so I had more time than the dancers with multiple roles that evening. The dressing room emptied once the show started.

I put on my black tights, a pair of warm slippers, and the saloon girl costume for *Frontiers* and found a corner to warm up backstage. While I stretched, I peeked around the back wing. The show was in progress, and I could see the dancers sweating. When they ran offstage, they'd collapse in exhaustion, take a few deep breaths, put their smile back on, and go out for more.

The curtain fell on the second ballet, and I went to the rosin box to put on my dyed black pointe shoes. I rubbed my heels in the yellow-white powder to prevent slipping.

The other *corps* girls sat and crowded in toward the box, so I hurried out of the way to tie my ribbons. Faye gave me a hand, and I stood and rolled up and down on my pointes to see how the shoes felt. She nodded her approval.

"Places, please," Greg, the stage manager, called, and the overture to *Frontiers* began. After weeks of rehearsal, the sound was an automatic cue to dance. I jogged in place to stay warm.

When I was little, I used to put on performances for my grandmother at her house. I'd go into her bathroom, try on all her makeup, and spritz my neck with her expensive perfume. She didn't mind, even when I put on one of her beautiful nightgowns for my "show" and tripped on the skirt, falling and ripping the sheer fabric.

Other women might have been mad, but my grandma clapped until her hands hurt. "Do it again. You were beautiful," she would say enthusiastically as she restarted the music. I would start over, leaping and waving my arms like a butterfly.

That excitement and pleasure remained with me as an eighteen-year-old about to make her professional debut. As a child, I was utterly confident my performance would please my audience, and that feeling lingered. Right before the curtain went up, something about the moment made me so excited. I knew I was bringing something good into people's lives. Grandma taught me that from an early age.

Faye squeezed my arm. "*Merde*," she said, a French curse word and the standard way dancers said good luck. All the ballet terminology was in French, so why shouldn't the slang be, too?

"*Merde*," I replied and hugged her.

"Break a leg, you two," Hilary said, putting her hands on our shoulders. Saying "break a leg" was considered bad luck in the theater, and as usual, Hilary rubbed me the wrong way.

Ryan was my partner. I could see him across the stage, kissing Rebecca in the wings. A minute later, Rebecca crossed over behind the backdrop so she and Allison could congregate with Faye and me. We checked each other's identical costumes and whispered *merdes*.

The four of us lined up in the second wing. On the count of eight, the four of us stepped down on the right foot. The new phrase of music began, and we marched onstage in unison, checking that we formed a perfect diagonal line. After four steps, we posed with our weight over our right pointe shoe. We put our right hands on our right knees and bent forward. As we arched our backs, we smiled at the audience. Adrenaline raced through my body.

Ryan, Marcus, Mikey, and Ian marched in from the opposite wing, synchronized and in line. Ryan faced me and posed with his arms crossed over his chest. The boys looked formidable in their spurs and cowboy hats. It was easy to smile at Ryan and interact with him onstage. He liked to perform as much as I did.

We danced, and I worked hard to stay in line and be on the music. Everything seemed to happen twice as fast as in rehearsal.

Out of the corner of my eye, I noticed William appear in the front wing. He stood so close to the edge that he was almost onstage. Even as I concentrated on my performance, I felt the acute awareness that William was there. He remained present in my mind's eye as I danced.

Our section ended, and Ryan held my hand as we ran offstage. "See you at the finale," he whispered. He squeezed my hand before letting go.

Faye was at the water cooler, and I went to get a drink. "How was it?" I asked. "It was OK, I think," Faye said. Her makeup already looked like it was melting off. "I didn't mess up," she said. "You?"

"So far, so good," I said, my addiction to the stage just beginning to bloom. I filled a paper cup with water and admired how happy everyone looked.

"There's so much energy out there," Faye whispered. A line of sweat dripped down her cheek.

I felt a rush of gratitude toward William.

We moved closer behind the second wing to watch. Four girls posed onstage in a perfect square. Natasha was the second movement principal, and her powerhouse style translated better onstage than in the studio. She traveled forward on her toes, flanked behind by the *corps*. In the performance, she had to tuck her pink tights into her pointe shoes, which made her legs look much longer than the black cutoff tights she usually wore in rehearsal.

Adam was Natasha's partner, and she was only a smidge shorter than him on *pointe*. I would never guess Adam was anywhere near forty from how he looked onstage, especially in a tasseled shirt and black cowboy hat. He seemed like a kid. The only giveaway was if I looked closely at his breathing, I could see dancing was more of an effort for him than the other men.

Natasha stepped forward with her leg behind her in *arabesque*, and Adam moved in to hold her waist. She raised her arm over her head, tossing her chin dramatically. A feather in her French twist went right up Adam's nose.

I couldn't help myself—I laughed. Faye giggled. "He's going to sneeze," Ryan said behind me. "Oh no. Please don't do it. Don't do it, man."

Adam walked Natasha around in a circle while she balanced on one foot. If he used his hand to move the feather, he would call the audience's attention, so he smiled and kept going.

"Adam won't sneeze," Lorenzo said, standing up from his stretch on the floor. "The man has been a principal dancer with LABT for over a decade. Professionalism. Watch it in action."

Lorenzo was right. Adam didn't sneeze even though we could all tell he was fighting the urge. "He looks like he might explode," Ryan said.

Natasha stepped away, and Adam's nose was free at last. "No sneeze," Lorenzo said. "Told you." Adam ran into the wing and gave Lorenzo a triumphant high-five.

"That was brutal," Adam said, laughing with us.

Natasha came off and put her hand on his shoulder. "We should have practiced with the headpiece," she said, laughing. "No matter, darling. You were magnificent." She kissed his cheek.

The second movement *corps* came offstage, and Faye and I backed up out of their way. "OK, cowboy," Ryan said to Lorenzo. "Show us something good out there." He lightly punched Lorenzo's arm.

"Don't worry, buddy," Lorenzo said, putting on his cowboy hat. He looked over at Faye and me and winked. "Watch and admire," he said.

Elizabeth balanced on her left leg onstage. Her reserved demeanor had disappeared, replaced by a playful attitude.

The eight *corps de ballet* boys and girls grinned as they posed in a diagonal line, making a tableau behind Elizabeth as her long right leg flew up repeatedly next to her ear. Their energy was contagious.

The audience clapped as she whirled across the floor and struck a pose near the wing, hands on her hips and one knee bent.

Lorenzo ran on. He winked at Elizabeth and launched into a showy series of consecutive turns and jumps, growling through clenched teeth. His sweat flew all over the stage.

"Ready?" Ryan asked. "Let's do it." He took my hand and led me to the back wing for the finale. Marcus brought Faye up behind us for the entrance. Mikey waved at me from the opposite wing while Rebecca held his other hand and jogged in place. Ian talked and gestured to Allison; she stared at him, bored.

The music changed, and we ran onstage on the new phrase, smiling at each other. We spaced ourselves evenly across, executed our sixteen counts of choreography, ran to the side, and posed.

The whole company was happy about the same thing at the same time. No one was angry about casting, depressed over their appearance, envious of someone else, or worried about the future. There was no time or energy to think of anything else while we danced. We dove into the final steps of the ballet, dripping in sweat and faces glowing. The stage shook under so many feet as we executed the choreography in unison.

Faye accidentally knocked me in the eye, and my fake eyelashes came unglued. I blinked and prayed they would hang on until the end. All I knew was that I had to keep dancing. Stay in line behind Natasha, I told myself. Keep going. Keep going.

Rebecca and Faye danced on either side of me, and I forced myself to stay even with them. The curtain fell on a frenzy of dancing as the music ended. Applause exploded over the final drum roll. I hurried to fix my eyelashes.

As the curtain flew back up, we snapped to place, and I bowed my head along with everyone else. When the curtain hit the ground again, people ran for the wings.

Ryan grabbed my hand and pulled me backward because we were the first group to bow. "They loved us, as usual," he whispered. "Congratulations. Now you're an official member of Los Angeles Ballet Theater."

"Thanks," I said, walking forward to curtsy.

The applause continued, and the soloists took their bows. I felt Ryan's free hand fiddling with the back of my costume. "Hey. Are you unhooking me? Should you do that?" I squeezed his hand.

"You'll get out faster," he said. I felt his warm breath on my neck.

"OK," I said, unsure if it was professional behavior to unhook a costume onstage.

Lorenzo led Elizabeth forward, their faces triumphant. The audience rose to its feet. "Bravo! Bravo!" people screamed. Someone threw a bouquet that landed at Elizabeth's feet. She picked it up and nodded her head graciously toward the crowd.

"Won't the audience notice if my costume falls open?" I whispered as Ryan worked more of the hooks open.

"Hate to break this to you," he said. "We're in the back row. No one looks at us." I glanced up at him, and he smiled amiably, oblivious that his comment hurt.

"Bravo! Bravo!" they shouted.

Lorenzo stepped back as Elizabeth ran to the wing to bring the maestro out on stage.

"When you're onstage, you never know who might be looking at you," I whispered.

The last hook on my costume popped open in his hand. "Yeah, your mother," he said.

There was a collective exhale as the curtain fell. Ryan stepped away from me. Dancers streamed past us, heading to the dressing room. I turned to follow the crowd and noticed that every *corps* costume hung open as we shuffled off the stage. Ryan was right. No one saw us.

Ryan caught up with Rebecca and put his arm around her shoulder as they walked offstage together. I followed, pulling pins out of my headpiece. Faye squeezed my hand. "We did it," she said.

The artistic staff was deep in conversation by the front wing.

It was like everyone lived life for the show. We trained to be extraordinarily self-aware, practicing the same movements daily for others to observe. As dancers, we were constantly on display, but we rarely spoke to the people watching us or made decisions at work, except about what we did with our bodies. We were great at following instructions.

And yet, I struggled with how invisible I felt. I longed to know that at least one person saw the real me. I wondered if our dancing said enough about what we had inside, and even if it did, did that matter if no one noticed?

CHAPTER 5

Elizabeth has been a principal here for a long time. William is infatuated with her. He admires and respects Adrienne and Natasha but doesn't seem as interested in them. Elizabeth had a boyfriend outside the company for a while, but that ended recently, and there are rumors that Lorenzo caused the breakup.

I can't say Elizabeth was supportive of my promotion. Natasha sure wasn't. Adrienne is the only one secure enough to say she was happy for me and that I deserved it. Elizabeth is generally lovely but hard to get to know, so people think she's stuck up. I think she worried I would get some of her roles.

Well, that didn't happen because I hurt myself, and since then, she's been a lot nicer to me. I don't want to think that's why, but she plays her cards very close to her chest.

Elizabeth: *"I've been fortunate. I moved to New York when I was fifteen and trained at the School of Ballet New York. I joined Ballet New York when I was seventeen and danced there for three years. It's cliché, but being in BNY was a dream come true.*

When William took over LABT, he asked me to join the company as a principal. I could tell by then that they would never promote me out of the corps *in New York. My family is in the Bay Area, too, so it made sense to be closer to them.*

William was so enthusiastic about my dancing. I didn't think much of myself in New York. Everyone there was talented, gorgeous, and unique, and it was impossible to stand out. But then, I came here and started dancing these notable roles immediately. I was only twenty-one.

I've had a problem with self-confidence. To know you were chosen to do something boosts your self-esteem because the staff believes in you. When I perform, it's just me. I can do what I want to do. That's helped me shake my fears and worry that people are looking at me to be a little more mature. Being a principal at LABT and working with William has been a blessing. One of my favorite things is getting flowers on opening night. That's a big deal because it symbolizes many things, especially your hard work. I hold those flowers, and I think, I earned this.

As younger people joined the company, I gained seniority and seasoning. I was more confident in my role as a principal dancer.

One interesting thing different from New York is how excited the younger generation here in Santa Monica is about ballet. The BNY audience is so old. Here, we're not hidden away behind security in a skyscraper. We have these store windows, making us accessible and exposing people to what we do.

I was passionate but never outgoing; I didn't know how to do the outreach except to the seniors who already knew they liked the ballet. William is good at it. That's always a challenge, getting younger people more interested in a classical art form. The thing with ballet that many people don't understand is that it's like being a professional athlete. There are few great ballet companies, particularly in the United States, so getting a spot in a big company is an honor.

For any dancer, it starts deep inside if they want a ballet career. You can't be pushed into dancing by a teacher or parent. It has to be all-consuming, because it's a grueling life, and it isn't worth it if it doesn't come from you. No matter how often you're told no, you can keep going if you believe in yourself. That perseverance through criticism gave me tremendous confidence."

All I saw of North Carolina during our visit was the hotel, the theater, and the closest restaurant. I was too tired to care. My skin was raw from the stage makeup, and I hated repeatedly putting all that stuff on and then rinsing it off two hours later. The hairspray refused to come out of my hair, even after three shampoos. My scalp ached from the countless bobby pins I used to hold my hair in place.

The more I performed, the more I could see that we were in the business of deception. I felt nothing like the effortless dancer the audience saw when I performed.

The bus dropped the company at the airport. People wandered off as soon as they checked their baggage at the curb, and I walked in with Carolyn since I sat with her on the bus. We split up at the magazine stand. I wanted food, and she was on a diet.

After downing a lousy airport bagel, I checked my watch and realized I was late for the plane. I ran for the gate, praying I hadn't been so careless as to miss the flight.

To my relief, the forty-four other dancers and the artistic staff were still there. William was talking to Natasha and Zif. I hurried over to where Faye sat in the terminal.

"When does our flight board?" I asked.

"Flight's delayed," Mikey said, looking up at me from his cross-legged position on the floor. "You can relax." He patted the floor next to him. "Your bag looks like it's going to explode. Why didn't you send more on the truck with the theater cases? They drive the sets; they might as well drive your other stuff, too."

"I did send my theater case," I said, embarrassed. "I just packed too much. This is my first tour. How was I supposed to know what I'd need?"

He laughed. "You'll learn."

"Have a seat," Faye said. I dropped my bag and sat between Ian and Kelly, who had a needle in her mouth while she stitched ribbons. Sewing pointe shoes was endless.

I stared out the window as we waited to board.

In Pittsburgh, I worked on my hair and makeup for an hour before my first performance of *Violins*. Before I went to the stage to put on my pointe shoes and stretch, I gave myself a long look in the mirror and thought, *don't screw this up.*

"*Merde*," Faye said, walking up to me in the wing as I did some *tendus*. She had the night off.

"Thanks. Do I look OK?" I looked down at my white leotard, skirt, and pink tights. It was such a simple and elegant costume. "I've never been onstage for twenty minutes nonstop. Every other ballet I've performed had exits. What if my nose starts to run?"

"Don't wipe it, whatever you do," Faye said. She pulled a loose string off my skirt. "I'm going out to the house to watch."

I wished I could see what I looked like from out front.

Allison and Rebecca practiced onstage in white costumes identical to mine. They both looked earnest. Hilary came barreling across the stage, practicing her *grande jetés*. Allison jumped out of the way and cursed.

"Do you think it's a bad sign that I'm not dancing tonight?" Faye asked. "Hilary said it was weird that I'm not in the show. Does that mean I won't get a *corps* contract?"

I peeled off my leg warmers and threw them under a table backstage. "You know better than to listen to Hilary," I said, covering up my worry. "Plenty of people aren't in every ballet."

Faye was the only person I trusted. It would be devastating if she didn't get a contract.

She hugged me and said, "I don't know how I would have gotten through the past few months without you."

"Five minutes. Five minutes, please," announced Greg over the loudspeaker. He peeked around the wing at Faye and me. "Did you hear that?" He was always meticulous.

"Yep," I said.

He nodded, adjusted his headset, and returned to his position in the front wing. William would be standing there in a few minutes when the performance began.

Faye left, and I walked back onstage to continue my warm-up. Adrienne and Zif practiced a lift near the curtain. He gently lowered her to the floor, and they whispered to each other softly, his hand on her lower back. The rest of the cast trickled onstage.

"Anna," Rebecca called. "Come here. We're having a huddle." She waved me over to where the dancers were congregating.

"We need our eighth girl," Allison said.

I joined the circle. Everyone linked hands, and I caught Hilary's eye. She gave me a half-smile.

"Wait for me," Adrienne said.

Allison dropped hands with Hilary to let Adrienne into the circle. Adrienne's presence felt like a comforting older sister.

Rebecca and Allison's hands were warm, and I could feel the energy in the group. We closed our eyes. In the dark, my breath synchronized with the others. We inhaled and exhaled as a team.

"*Merde*," Adrienne said as we opened our eyes.

"Places, please," Greg called from the front wing.

I walked to my place on stage left. Three girls lined up directly in front of me at the quarter mark. On stage right, the other four formed an identical line.

Allison was my opposite, and she caught my eye across the stage. "I'll watch you out of my peripheral vision. Try to stay directly across from me. We sometimes get out of line in rehearsals," she said.

"OK," I said, by now used to the way Allison was always telling people what to do.

Greg's voice boomed over the loudspeaker. "Good evening, ladies and gentlemen. Welcome to this evening's performance. At this time, we ask that you turn off all pagers and cell phones. We would also like to remind you that taking flash photographs is not permitted. Thank you. Enjoy the show."

I faced the curtain with my left foot flat in front of my right foot. My toes pointed out into the wings. As I inhaled, I placed my arms in a perfect circle with my fingertips in front of my thighs. I pulled up every muscle in my calves, knees, thighs, rear, and stomach. At the same time, I pushed my shoulders down and lengthened my neck without swaying my back.

The seven other girls prepared their bodies, too. Each of us had individual physical intricacies we'd navigated through the years of daily practice.

In the wing, Adrienne and Zif pressed their foreheads together for a moment. Their partnership was unlike anyone else's and came from their deep connection. They were mesmerizing together.

The curtain went up. I saw the conductor illuminated by a tiny light on the music stand. He raised his baton.

All eight of us bent our knees and launched into the opening steps. The music sounded powerful and immediate.

We danced into a circle formation and opened out into a line. I took Adrienne's hand. She smelled like sweat and perfume. I turned to let my arm wrap around my torso as I stepped back to face the audience. On the next count, Adrienne offered her other hand to Rebecca, who mirrored my movements on Adrienne's other side.

I looked at the people in the front row. The few faces I could make out looked deep in thought. Rebecca, Adrienne, and I stood there, locked in our chain of arms for one full count. As the music climbed, we raised our right legs behind us to create a chain of *arabesques*. It was my favorite moment in the ballet.

Rebecca and I rejoined the *corps*. We linked hands and shifted into two lines of four. In unison, we traveled downstage on pointe. Everyone bent their knees and jumped. My legs crisscrossed three times in the air. I landed on my right knee at the exact moment the music came to an end.

Applause. The curtain fell. I looked over my hand into the front wing and stared directly into William's eyes.

Faye greeted me as I came out of the shower in my towel. "You've got to watch from the audience," Faye said. Her face glowed. "I was blown away."

"Was I OK?" I asked.

"Adrienne and Zif were unbelievable," Faye said. "Try to keep your shoulders down. They tend to creep up when you get tired."

I missed the days when my ballet teachers corrected me. If Lila or William gave us feedback, it was always about the choreography or something stylistic, not our technique. They didn't have time or energy when there were so many ballets to assemble. We were professionals because we had the basics figured out, but I'd spent my life relying on teachers to help refine my dancing. I missed that support.

Everyone was tired and hungry when we left the theater. The shows drained away energy but left me with a sense of accomplishment. Every time I performed, I wanted to do it more.

George arranged for a restaurant to stay open late for us since almost everyone preferred to eat a bigger meal after the show. We needed to be able to hold our stomachs in while we danced. I ate only a little before a performance, but often, everything closed by the time we left the theater. Eating disorders were a cliché in ballet, but it was impossible to do the job without food.

Two days later, we flew from Pittsburgh to New Jersey. I had a performance off, so I could finally watch from the front. Faye wasn't dancing either. We sat in the audience together on opening night. The ballets and the dancers looked different from the house.

Down in the audience, I saw how the dancers' facial expressions came across onstage. Personality quirks appeared in how people moved. Mikey had sloppy technique and a sleepy smile. Ian looked like he was performing on a

Disney cruise ship. Ryan came across as energetic and charming. Allison's movements were harsh, and she made angry faces. Rebecca floated through choreography like her mind was far away.

The principals looked more mature. Lorenzo was huge and the most masculine presence in the company. Elizabeth came across as elegant yet vulnerable. Jeff was intimidating and remote. Natasha was overconfident to the point of rudeness. And Adrienne and Zif looked like royalty. They were all formidable. My hands hurt from clapping when the curtain fell for the last time.

"I wonder what Kelly did tonight," Faye said as we crossed the street back to the hotel. "Did you know she's only performing in one show of *Tidal Moods* for the rest of the tour? She's here in case someone gets injured, but that's it."

Kelly was in a tough professional situation. The apprentices shouldn't have been dancing more than a senior *corps* member; in her case, we were.

"She left at half-hour, before the show started," I said.

"Why would the company hire someone and not put them onstage?" Faye asked. "The casting makes no sense to me. Allison does three *corps* roles in one night when Kelly doesn't perform. The less Kelly dances, the more out of shape she gets."

I said, "I wonder if that's William's choice or Lila's."

"Mikey said that William tells Lila which *corps* dancers he likes, and she does all the *corps* casting," Faye said. "William only casts the principals."

"It's good the hotel is so close," I said. "Kelly was stuck at the theater in North Carolina. Here, if someone gets hurt or sick, it would only take five minutes for her to run over." If we were off and left at half-hour, it was in our contract that we had to be close enough to get to the theater and be onstage in thirty minutes if someone became sick or got injured.

We both yawned as we stepped into the elevator.

"Press seven," Faye said.

From down the hall, a male voice called, "Hold the elevator, please."

I put my hand in the doors, and William squeezed through.

"Good evening," he said, and we nodded politely. "Fifth floor, please. Very nice job tonight, ladies." He still had his black tuxedo on from the evening's performance, and his bow tie hung undone around his neck. He ran his hand through his thick silver hair.

The memory of his eyes fixed on mine at the end of *Violins* burned in my head. Faye pressed five and studied the floor numbers over the elevator door.

"Thank you," I replied, realizing William didn't know that Faye and I hadn't performed. The doors opened on the fifth floor.

"Good night," he said, stepping out.

The elevator closed, and William disappeared.

"Well, then," I said.

"At least he said, 'Good job.'" Faye laughed cynically.

I unlocked the door to our hotel room. "Does he even remember who we are?"

The question hung over me as we put on our pajamas and crawled into bed.

If I wanted to move up in the company, I needed to make sure William at least knew whether I'd been on the stage.

CHAPTER 6

*K*elly has only been in the company a year and is one of the youngest dancers in the corps de ballet. *Her technique is relatively weak, but she has a beautiful stage presence and an unusually confident demeanor for someone her age. She also knows every count in every ballet, so the other girls always ask her to go over the choreography with them. Many people think she'll have a significant career here, but I'd be surprised if she makes it out of the* corps. *She's not cutthroat enough.*

Kelly: *I've been in a relationship with ballet for most of my life. I'm from a small town in Virginia, and my small studio was only ten minutes from my house. I studied there since I was two. I'm the only Black dancer in the company and the only one who didn't come from a big, famous ballet institution. William taught a master class in Washington, D.C., when I was seventeen, and my mom drove me into the city to take it. Afterward, I asked him if he was hiring. He said he would consider me for an apprenticeship if I flew to LA and took classes with the company. So I did, and he offered me a job.*

I like being in LABT, but I know I'm missing out. Our lives are so sheltered. William doesn't notice me much. He's probably glad I'm here to be a solid corps *member, but he's certainly not taken with me like he is with Elizabeth and others. If I knew how to catch his eye, I would. We all think that maybe, one day, he'll suddenly look at us differently and say, 'Wow, she deserves more.' It's how we keep ourselves going, that hope. It's not true. How he sees us from the beginning is probably how he'll always see us.*

The ballet season opened in Los Angeles in November, and before every show, William gave a free pre-performance talk. The hard-core patrons rushed to the ballet early to see him in the flesh. They savored his every word.

His voice boomed over the loudspeaker into our dressing room on opening night. "Roizman's point of departure for *Rhapsody* was the first American ballerinas who inspired him," he told the audience. "It was the first ballet he choreographed in the West."

"He milks these Roizman stories for all they're worth," Kelly said, rolling her eyes. To everyone's relief, they'd cast her in the matinées that weekend. When one person in the *corps* suffered, it affected everyone's morale.

William continued, "From there, our program segues into *Georgia on My Mind*. The point of departure for this piece is the nostalgia we feel for specific places . . ."

"If William doesn't stop overusing that 'point of departure' phrase, I'm going to scream," said Allison.

I laughed, smudging my eye shadow while trying to apply it. Their mocking was all in good fun. Everyone knew William's star power kept the money coming in.

Allison flipped her hair over her head and brushed it into a ponytail. She was even crankier than usual because she wasn't first cast in one of the season opener ballets.

Everyone's emotions, including mine, depended on casting. The stakes were higher for a senior *corps* dancer like Allison. While Faye and I were grateful we had one performance of one tiny part for the whole weekend, Allison was furious if she danced every night but wasn't first cast for everything.

I turned up the music on my headphones and studied my reflection. In half an hour, the tired, pale girl in the mirror would be smiling, made-up, and ready to go.

The loudspeaker crackled. "Now I'd like to open it up to questions," we heard William say to the crowd. This part was interesting; we always liked hearing what the audience asked.

"What are the dancers' day jobs?" asked a man. "What do they do in real life?"

"No!" Rebecca said. "Someone did not just ask that."

"Ballet is their day job," William said with a sigh. "Our dancers rehearse and perform eight hours a day, six days a week." He handled the answer graciously, although we knew the question irked him, too.

"William, when will you perform with the company?" a woman asked.

Allison snorted.

"I don't think you want to see a sixty-year-old man up there in tights, so that won't happen anytime soon," he said. "Thanks for asking." He enjoyed that kind of attention, and even though we couldn't see him, we knew he was smiling.

"Why does your company focus so much on Roizman ballets?" asked another man. "Many of us want to see a classic like *Swan Lake*."

"Oh, brother," said Kelly. "William hates that subject."

"My background is in Roizman ballets," William said. "Not to mention that a production of *Swan Lake* with full sets and costumes costs much more than a production of *Tidal Moods*. The dancers in *Tidal Moods* wear leotards and tights. There are no sets. But I love a good *Swan Lake* as much as the next guy. Let me know if you want to finance a production."

There was a long stretch of laughter.

Faye said, "People don't understand how much money these productions cost or how hard we work. No wonder ballet companies are broke."

"At least there are people who support us," I said. "The arts always have trouble. Poverty comes with the territory."

A woman in the audience gushed, "Oh William, I remember when you danced the lead in *Fire*. You were like a dream. It's such an honor to see you in person. Do any of the up-and-coming dancers in LABT have that certain, you know, *je ne sais quoi*?"

The dressing room fell silent. I remembered one of my first ballet teachers, Madame Androvichevsky, who had a thick Russian accent. She used to tell my mother, "Anna vil be prima. She vil never be in ze *corps*," and my mom had quoted her many times over the years, hanging on that line as a mantra or just a reassurance that we were going through all the stress, heartache, and expense for a good reason. If my mom or a dolly-dinkle ballet teacher said something like that, the comment was sweet but could be dismissed. All of us had heard that from our mothers and early teachers.

A prediction of greatness from William, however, now that would mean something.

"We have many talented dancers," William said. "You'll have to watch and pick your favorites this season. I have my eye on a few." He paused, and we waited, hoping he would be more explicit. But he knew better.

"Come on, William," Hilary said, speaking up for the first time. "Name names."

The older dancers looked at her, surprised. Hilary wasn't friendly like Faye and me, and rarely talked to people at work.

"Thank you for coming today," he finally said. "I hope you enjoy this evening's program." The audience applauded politely, and the noise over the intercom reverted to gentle voices and instruments tuning. There was a collective—and audible—exhale in the dressing room.

The company traveled to Palm Springs for the weekend, and I took a barre spot onstage by Ryan for company class. "Aah, Palm Springs," Ryan mused, resting his elbows on the portable barre. "The last time we did *Fire* at this theater, an ambulance was in the parking lot after the show. The ballet was so exciting we gave someone a heart attack."

"For real?" I asked.

He gave me his most charming smile. "Would I make that up?"

Class and tech rehearsal rushed past. I was in *Violins* and *Frontiers*. At half-hour, I already had my makeup and hair done. Faye sat beside me in the dressing room, staring at her reflection. She looked tired.

Suddenly, Ian barged into the dressing room. "You won't believe what just happened," he said.

"Hey!" said Rebecca. "What if some of us weren't dressed?"

"Whatever," Ian snapped. "I'm gay. Besides, this is important." I had never seen him look so serious about anything, and a sick feeling rushed through my stomach. "What's wrong?" I asked.

The pre-performance rituals ground to a halt. We were used to Ian coming into our dressing room, but everyone could tell by his voice and facial expression that for once he wasn't there to watch us do our hair.

"There was an accident," Ian said. "We were outside smoking and saw the whole thing. One second, a guy is crossing the street. The next, he's lying limp in the middle of the road."

"What are you talking about?" asked Faye, snapping out of her reflection-induced trance. I put down my hairbrush.

"We were outside for the pre-show cigarette," Ian said. "A guy cut across the major street behind the theater. We were far away, so he was just a silhouette, but he had a backpack, probably a college kid. A huge truck barreled around the corner out of nowhere. The driver didn't see him. Elizabeth screamed so loud I went deaf in one ear."

"You're joking, right?" Rebecca asked.

"It's true," he said. "We watched the whole thing. Lorenzo took off running to try and give him CPR before the ambulance came."

"When did this happen?" I asked.

"Now," he said. "I ran in here right away. I was too scared to follow Lorenzo over there. Everyone's congregating outside." He gestured for us to follow him out of the dressing room.

The regular smokers were already gathered in the hall. Mikey held Kelly in a protective hug, and her torso practically disappeared into his chest. Jeff was talking fast and gesturing dramatically to Allison. The door at the end of the hall flew open, and Lorenzo came walking in. Elizabeth rushed to him. "Are you OK?" she asked.

"The ambulance took him away," Lorenzo said, "but he was already dead. He never knew what hit him."

"The medics confirmed he wasn't breathing?" Elizabeth asked.

"Fifteen minutes, boys and girls," Greg interrupted over the loudspeaker. "This is your fifteen-minute call."

Ten minutes later, the curtain went up. Even death couldn't intrude on our jobs. People paid to see the show, no matter what happened in the outside world, and we were professionals.

I gave a solid performance of *Violins*. My body moved soundlessly through the choreography, using the dance as a vessel for my shock.

The *Nutcracker* grind began the day after Thanksgiving, making it impossible for most of us to go home for the holiday. Kelly invited Faye, Ian, Mikey, and me over for dinner at her place, and she cooked the turkey.

Ian was right: *Nutcracker* may have been fun to dance in as a kid, but as a company member, it was a circus. I had been in the *Nutcracker* since I was nine and knew I'd always feel nostalgic about it, but *Nutcracker* as a company member was a different experience.

On opening night, I sat on the couch onstage before the curtain went up. Dressed like an army general for the opening party scene, Ryan walked over and said, "Lookin' good, Grandma." His fake mustache hung crookedly off his upper lip.

The taller girls played the mothers in the party scene and wore beautiful gowns, but not me. The heavy makeup and silver wig made me look like an eighty-year-old woman.

"You know they like you if they think you have what it takes to be Grandma on opening night," Ryan teased.

When the overture began, I stood in the wings. A little girl in ringlets and a pink dress came up to me. She was probably ten and played the role of the grandchild. "Are you my grandmother?" she asked.

"I'm the youngest grandma you'll ever have," I said. She laughed and skipped over to her friend. I remembered being that girl. Her eager face, brimming with potential, was one of the reasons I loved the *Nutcracker*. She'd have lifelong memories.

Mikey appeared just in time for the cue. We hobbled onstage. Our choreography involved sitting on the couch and smiling at the children. As soon as we sat down, Mikey pretended to fall asleep.

A little boy threw up onstage during the soldier dance. Many of us gagged. It was also hard not to laugh, especially when Hilary, the maid, had to go over and clean it up. She looked ready to vomit as she hurried offstage with puke on the bottom of her apron.

The Grandfather's Dance marked the end of the party scene. Mikey led me to center stage for our few counts of shuffling. I kissed my "grandkids" goodbye and shuffled into the wing, anxious for what came next.

Offstage, I ripped my wig off. People cleared out of my way as I rushed down the stairs. The *corps* girls stayed far from the stage, and the character shoes for the grandma costume made it hard to run fast.

By the time I reached the dressing room, I had removed all my accessories. A female dresser unhooked the purple dress while I frantically scrubbed off my old lady makeup. The costume fell to the floor, and I stepped out of the skirt. The new layer of makeup to make me young again went on next. I raced to fix my bun, where the wig had messed up my hair. The rest of the *corps* was already upstairs for the Snow scene. I heard the Fight scene music over the intercom and knew time was running out.

With only a few minutes to go, I jammed pins into my tiara to anchor it to my head, put on my pointe shoes, changed my earrings, put on my silver tutu, waited for the dresser to hook my costume, and ran for the stairs. When I appeared in the wing, the snow was already falling onstage. I was cold, panicked, and miserable but had made it.

Allison led my line of snowflakes onstage. Paper snow flew up my nose and down my throat. I held on to my silver wands with a death grip. Faye dropped one of her wands, and Kelly kicked it offstage.

In the second act, I switched costumes between the Spanish Dance, the Waltz of the Flowers, and then back to my Spanish outfit again for the finale. By the time Clara and the Prince flew away in the sled, I had used up every ounce of energy. I was as tired from the constant identity change as the dancing.

After showering and putting on street clothes, Faye and I left the dressing room together. As we reached the exit, Greg, the stage manager, hurried over. "Anna," he said, "you have a fan letter."

He handed me a folded note, scribbled on the back of a program. "Someone dropped this off right after the curtain came down. He said he couldn't stay but wanted you to know he was here."

"Thanks," I said. Greg nodded and hurried back to the crew.

"Open it," Faye urged. I unwrapped the note.

Hey Anna,

You looked splendid tonight. It's a relief that you've recovered from the tree branch attack. I came with my family. I'm sorry we couldn't stay to talk to you in person. Happy holidays.

Ethan

We had nothing in common. I crumpled the note and dropped it in the trash.

On Christmas Eve, I stood onstage before the curtain rose on our twentieth performance of *Nutcracker*. We'd given two performances a day for the past two weeks. Ryan walked over in his army general costume, his mustache still hanging crooked off his upper lip. The performance ran like a machine by this point in the run. How did the Broadway stars perform the same thing night after night? I'd grown bored with the whole show.

Backstage, there was a festive atmosphere, and I had gone a little crazy on the makeup. If I crossed my eyes, I could see the giant mole I had painted on my nose. I had even glued a few eyelash hairs in it.

"Forester. That's repulsive," Ryan said, chuckling.

"Not any worse than this." I held up my right hand, which had a sixth finger. "I found this fake finger at a Halloween store." We grinned at each other.

Mikey appeared dressed for Grandpa. "Here we go again," he said, bowing and leading me into the wing as the overture began.

As the party scene continued, Hilary, as the maid, carried on a tray of drinks for the choreographed toast. For Christmas Eve, Ian had filled them with champagne.

Allison played Marie's mother, and she held my arm as I tottered over to the couch. Ryan took my purse and fiddled with it behind the sofa before placing it on Mikey's seat beside me.

"What are you doing?" I asked Ryan, who ignored me.

Mikey sat down a moment later, and the whoopee cushion inside deflated with a bang, right in time to the music. Ian, Ryan, and Rebecca were close enough to hear it and erupted with laughter. William and Lila were in the wings as I rushed off for my quick change.

At intermission, we were giddy with anticipation for the holiday, and the dressing room buzzed with energy.

"Christmas Eve is always my favorite *Nutcracker* performance," Kelly said as she pinned in her headpiece for Waltz of the Flowers.

The door to the dressing room flew open, and Lila walked in. It was a rare appearance. She always spoke to us onstage, never while we were changing. Most of us spent the intermission picking paper snow out of our hair, and the last thing we wanted to deal with was a member of the artistic staff.

"This is a professional ballet company," Lila said. "You do not have the right to take liberties with the party scene. If anything like that happens again, someone's getting fired." The threat hung in the air as she glared around the room. My mouth twitched, but I knew the worst thing I could do at that moment was laugh. I bit the inside of my cheek, ashamed.

I don't know how we had developed the urge to challenge Lila's authority. Maybe because *Nutcracker* burned everyone out, we had reached the point of not caring. Lila was smart enough to know she'd lost control. We'd been inappropriately silly and unprofessional. It was beneath us.

The second act was a much more somber affair. We knew the rules, but at the end of the day, sometimes, we still needed to act like kids.

I flew home to Rock Island for five days after *Nutcracker*. All I did was eat, sleep, and read Karina's journal. My parents' presence had a comforting effect. Sometimes, I didn't realize how exhausted I was until I stopped dancing for a few days.

Adrienne is hard to get to know because she and Zif live in their private world. I was surprised at what she told me since she's always upbeat in public. I would never have guessed she felt insecure sometimes, too.

Adrienne: *"I'm still not always sure I'm cut out for ballet. I could stand to have longer legs and better feet. I wouldn't have kept going if I hadn't had Zif during my early years. He pushed me forward and believed in me during many seasons when I felt like giving up. Love and support go a long way in this career, and I can't imagine how so many dancers do it when they're single and far away from their families. I'd be so lonely without Zif."*

We opened *Elements* in Los Angeles in January. *Elements* had three sections: *Earth*, *Wind*, and *Fire*, which were sometimes performed separately, but I loved them combined in the full-length program. On my birthday, I danced in the corps of *Fire* for the first time. *Fire* was still my favorite ballet, and the lead was still my dream role, the one I understudied but didn't get to perform in the SBNY workshop. I was just thrilled to be in the *corps*. The choreography was even more fun to dance than it was to watch.

I studied Adrienne and Zif from the wings as they performed the *Fire pas de deux*. Their lives looked so perfect. I couldn't understand how someone as incredible as Adrienne could feel the way Karina described in her journal. It was the saddest thing I'd ever heard. If even Adrienne couldn't feel adequate, how could I hope to be good enough?

In the middle of March, George announced that next season's contracts were going out in the mail. Faye and I were a wreck all week.

"No one has said a word to me about how I did this year," Faye said, flipping through mindless television shows.

"I have no idea if William or Lila likes me either," I said from the kitchen, putting brownies in the oven.

Faye said, "All we knew is that they let us perform."

A few days later, she pulled the envelopes out of the mailbox. My hands shook when I reached to take mine. "If you don't get a *corps* contract, what's your plan?" Faye asked.

The thought made me sick. "It's too late to audition for other companies for next season. I'd have to move home and try to stay in shape for nine months or revisit my deferral to the University of Chicago. What would you do?"

"No idea," she said. "This year has been so hard I can't think beyond the next day. Let's find out."

We ripped open our envelopes. To my relief, I saw my name on a full-fledged *corps de ballet* contract. When I raised my eyes to meet Faye's, she smiled. We had both made it.

"Congrats," Ian said across the barre before class. "I heard you, Faye, and Hilary are coming back. You deserve it."

"Thanks," I said, tying my pointe shoes.

In a quieter voice, Ian said, "William forced Adam to retire."

"I was hoping that wouldn't happen," I said. It was so sad for Adam to leave that way.

Ian was less emotional about it. "It's better than William letting Adam dance past his expiration date. He wants the audiences to remember him in his prime."

"I guess." A few other *corps* dancers who had lost momentum were leaving, too. I looked around the room at them, quietly tying the ribbons on their pointe shoes. I felt like I didn't know them and couldn't imagine making that decision.

It was amazing how the hierarchy could change so quickly. In the company, we were whatever William said we were.

Soon, in the outside world, the dancers who were leaving could be whatever they wanted.

The company contract didn't mean I had financial security. The season lasted only thirty-five weeks out of the year, and we were unemployed for the remaining seventeen weeks. In Europe, most dancers danced all year and didn't have layoffs. They were lucky to have such steady jobs. We and other companies in the United States had to collect unemployment during the breaks.

The energy at work lagged the last few weeks of the season. The dancers were more carefree in class and rehearsals, like kids about to end the school year.

Faye and I packed up our apartment. The nine-month lease was up, and we had decided to get our own places. We both needed somewhere to get away from work, and separate rents were doable since we'd both be in the *corps* next season and making a little more money.

Allison and I were the last ones in the dressing room on the final day.

"What are your plans during the layoff?" I asked.

Allison said, "The usual. My family only lives an hour away, so I'll visit them for a few days, and then I'm road-tripping to Seattle with some old friends."

"Do you ever get another job?" I asked, voicing the question that had weighed on my mind. I would be in Rock Island for three weeks, taking classes at my old ballet school and hoping they'd let me try teaching for the first time. But other than that, the long break was a question mark.

"I tried to get a job my first year," she said. "It was a waste. Making coffee paid less than unemployment, and I needed time to take classes. Just because we're laid off doesn't mean we don't need to keep up our technique. Lila gets mad if we return out of shape. The principals are lucky and usually have gigs lined up. Miss one day, and you know. Two days your teacher knows. Three, everyone knows."

"Ouch," I said, knowing she was right.

CHAPTER 7

When I returned from Rock Island, my layoff days in L.A. started with morning ballet class. The senior company members took turns teaching during the break, depending on who was in town. In the afternoon, I went to the beach and swam; at night, I read novels or hung out with whichever *corps* friends were around. The slower pace was a welcome change, even if I felt anxious from time to time about what I was doing with my life.

I decorated my new apartment, a first. One of the dancers who left to join a company in Europe at the end of last season sold me her overstuffed chenille couch. I bought a round wood table and chairs, a sleigh bed, and framed black and white photography—mostly various city shots—to hang on the walls.

On the first day back to work, I stopped at the bulletin board to check the schedule, which they usually posted a day in advance. Because it was the first day, I came in without any advance notice of what the day held. There was a rehearsal for *Afternoon Symphony* at noon that listed every *corps* girl's name except mine.

"Allen, Forester," appeared next to the two-thirty *Afternoon Symphony* rehearsal. *Afternoon Symphony* wasn't on the performance schedule until the end of February, eight months away, but we would be spending our first month back learning all the new ballets for the season. Then we'd have months to forget them once performances began.

"Allen" meant Natasha Allen, so I was called to a rehearsal at lunchtime with a principal, and Natasha scared me. Her conversations I'd overheard were either inappropriate jokes or a litany of complaints. I wasn't even sure she knew my name.

I had seen *Afternoon Symphony* once during my first year at SBNY. It was a Roizman ballet with twelve *corps* girls, a principal couple, and one female soloist. The soloist role was all complicated footwork and impressive leaps. It was precisely the kind of part they always cast Natasha in because she had a huge jump and beautiful feet.

After class, I had two hours off because all the other girls stayed for the *Afternoon Symphony corps* rehearsal. It was my first day as a full member of the *corps de ballet*, and it felt strange not to be at the rehearsal with all my peers.

I passed by Hilary as I was leaving the studio. "Have a nice break," she said, giving me an icy look.

At two twenty-five, I walked into one of the small studios and started to warm up. Natasha appeared at two thirty-one.

"So, William wants you to learn the soloist part," she said, putting down her bag. "He likes you."

My mouth was dry as I took off my legwarmers. The fact was, this one rehearsal had made a lot of people mad. There were dancers like Allison who'd spent ten years in the *corps de ballet* and were still waiting to dance their first soloist role.

William hadn't shown particular interest in me the season before. This special treatment landed in my life like a bomb. I couldn't process what it all meant.

"It's been a few years since I danced this," Natasha said, switching on the screen at the front of the room so we could watch the opening to *Afternoon Symphony*. She was the soloist in the film. "I think this performance is from four years ago," she said, pulling her hair back into her usual ponytail.

After we watched her section, Natasha walked to the center of the room to start teaching me the steps. I followed and stood behind her.

"You have eight counts to walk in," she said. The time flew as we worked through each step and count of the choreography. She taught me the entire role in fifty minutes, and right before our time was up, she asked, "Want to run it for me once?"

My brain felt overwhelmed with musical counts, arm positions, and the sequence of the steps. When I learned *corps* roles, at least I could confer about the choreography or go over counts with my friends. Not now. I was on my own.

I walked to the back of the studio, and Natasha hit play on the recording. We counted to eight together. I danced the role for her the best I could.

When I finished, she nodded and stopped the music. "Not bad," she said, looking pleasantly surprised. "You'll have to practice the *brisés*. At least now it's in your head."

I nodded and practiced a few more *brisés*, a small jump where I crossed my back leg in front of my front leg, bending over my extended legs in the air.

I thanked her and left the studio, confident I could work hard and do the part well. My legs weren't as powerful as Natasha's, but my jump was light and would bring a different quality to the choreography. It was a luxury not to have to worry about staying in line. I would be able to show off what made my dancing special.

Rebecca invited me to lunch the next day. We picked an outdoor café and basked in the nice weather. I told her how happy I was about her promotion to soloist. She congratulated me on my *corps* contract and the *Afternoon Symphony* opportunity. We talked about our layoffs and which movies we'd seen.

"It's huge to be someone William likes," Rebecca said after our food arrived.

I knew she didn't mean to make a dig, but I felt like she was testing me.

"Were you nervous when you did your first soloist role?" I asked, remembering how well she'd done as lead Marzipan in *Nutcracker*.

Rebecca said, "William stood right in the front wing. Everyone was watching. I had plenty of rehearsal and felt prepared. I worked hard and tried to be in the moment and savor it. That's what performing is: being in the moment every second we're out there. It's not about who can do the steps. Any of us who makes it this far has the technique and can execute. We're talking about what it means to go to the next level. People live through us when we're onstage, and it's our job to make watching worth their time."

I nodded, reading between the lines. Responsibility came along with the opportunity, and it was up to me to prove I deserved it.

"Once you perform a soloist role, you have to become more than just a dancer," Rebecca said, sipping her iced tea. "This experience will help you grow as an artist. Dancers in the *corps* learn how to stay in line, blend in, and be a part of something larger than just their dancing. But principals are artists on another level. Honestly, I was only afraid before I walked onstage. Once you're out there, you can't care about other people's opinions. If I took all the negative things people said about my dancing to heart, I wouldn't be here now."

"I worry that I'm not good enough," I admitted.

"Get over it. That's not your concern, and it's not for you to decide," she said. "All you get is the knowledge that William picked you. He could choose any of us. There are plenty of others waiting—"

"I know—"

"You're the one he picked," she said. "You're a natural on stage. Even as an apprentice, you stood out in the *corps*. Just work hard and wait. Don't care too much if the others hate you. There will be a long time when you feel like nothing comes together, and then one day, it will. William knows what he's doing. He's been in this business a long time."

Once the rehearsal period ended and I was back onstage dancing in the *corps de ballet,* the fall flew by quickly. After a grueling *Nutcracker* run, I spent New Year's in L.A. and went out with my friends. It wasn't until early January that we had a complete rehearsal of *Afternoon Symphony.*

"We'll run the first cast to start," Lila said, her pen and paper poised to note every mistake. "If there's time, we'll run the second group."

I stretched on the side while the *corps* danced the opening, wondering if there would be time for me to try the soloist role. Natasha was first cast, and I marked behind her in the back of the room when her entrance came. I didn't have much space, so I concentrated on my arm positions.

William strode into the room during the first cast run-thru and took a seat in the front by Lila. He crossed his arms and stared intently while Adrienne and Zif danced the *pas de deux*.

The energy in the room grew intense with William's arrival. The rehearsals were more like a performance when he came. Lila inspired fear because she yelled at us, but William commanded respect.

The first cast finished the run-through with ten minutes to spare. "Second cast, from the top," Lila said. "Elizabeth and Jeff in the *pas de deux*. Anna as the soloist."

My nerves were worse than before an actual performance.

The *corps* girls danced the opening while I jogged in place. My heart pounded. When the soloist music began, I walked forward and posed in the center of the room. I had never danced front and center with the company. Everyone was watching. It was the first time many dancers had paid attention to me since I joined the company.

I had thought about the role frequently over the past six months. At night in bed, I visualized it before I fell asleep.

When I ate dinner alone in my apartment, I watched the video. Except for Natasha, no one had seen any of my work to prepare.

I danced the choreography I had studied diligently and internalized. William watched me closely. The movements weren't entirely comfortable, and I became painfully exhausted halfway through. Thinking about and marking the steps was different than dancing the role completely without stopping. By the end, I felt myself slipping behind the music. My mind understood the role, but my body didn't have the stamina yet.

When my first section ended, I walked off the floor and tried to catch my breath. Faye smiled at me encouragingly. I did my best to appear confident, but inside, I was nervous, longing for approval. To hide my anxiety, I made a production of stretching out my calves while the *corps* finished the section. I glanced out the window, and to my amazement, there was Ethan.

He waved, but I was in another world. The last thing I needed at that moment was an intrusion.

I went on for my second entrance and danced.

"Pretty good, Anna," Lila said, stopping the music at the end of my part. "Let's talk about those *brisés*." She beckoned me to her to go over corrections. I braved a glance at William, and he gave me the briefest of smiles. A moment later, his expression turned as impassive as ever.

After the rehearsal, I walked closer to the window to see if Ethan was still there. He was gone.

Before my debut in *Afternoon Symphony*, I was called to rehearse a new ballet. The dancers at the first rehearsal of *Spring Season Pas de Deux* included Adrienne, Zif, Elizabeth, Lorenzo, Jeff, and me.

The other two partnerships were long-established, so Jeff and I looked at each other, knowing we'd be paired. He pursed his lips and turned away.

I was, conspicuously, the only *corps* member at the rehearsal, and Natasha was the only principal woman not called.

"William choreographed *Spring Season Pas de Deux* his first year as director," Adrienne told me.

Lila walked into the room and clapped her hands. "Let's go. Ladies enter first." She ran her hand through her short hair and turned to inspect herself in the mirror. Zif, Lorenzo, and Jeff moved to the side of the room.

Adrienne, Elizabeth, and I marked behind Lila as she showed us the steps. Our qualities were so different: Adrienne's warmth, Elizabeth's glamour, and my, I didn't know. What did I have to offer? Why was I here instead of Natasha?

"Now, let's add in your partners," Lila said. She put her hands on my shoulders and positioned me next to Jeff. He crossed his arms and glared.

William appeared in the doorway near the end of the rehearsal, and he and Lila took a moment to whisper. Adrienne explained some of the counts and helped me review the steps while we waited for Lila to return.

Before he left, William turned to us and said, "Remember, this piece is about first love. Youth and innocence." His eyes scanned the room. I turned to examine my reflection in the mirror, feeling a rush of confidence about his request. So that's what I was. Next to Adrienne and Elizabeth, I most embodied the qualities he'd asked for.

But how were Jeff and I supposed to act like we were in love?

The third rehearsal scheduled for *Spring Season Pas de Deux* caused even more gossip because Jeff and I were the only ones called. Natasha and Allison whispered and glared at me all through class. Even Faye, Kelly, and Rebecca kept their distance.

William might as well have put a target on my back. Many dancers spent ten years in the *corps* and never danced any featured parts. I worked hard, was never sick or injured, and danced the best I could daily, but I hadn't done more than anyone else.

Jeff was warming up at the barre when I arrived for the rehearsal.

We exchanged nods, but his disdain was immediately palpable. His brown hair and pale skin matched my coloring, and he was shorter than Lorenzo and Zif, so I could see why William decided we were well-matched. Jeff, however, looked like he'd prefer anyone other than me.

Lila arrived with a curt smile. "Let's run it and see how it goes," she said.

Jeff and I began the *pas de deux*. Lila watched, letting the tape run. We rehearsed the entire opening. I remembered the partnering classes at ballet school, how I used to dance with friends, and we'd joke and have a good time together. Jeff was so cold.

He guided me awkwardly through the supported turns and small lifts. I sensed he didn't want to touch me and wouldn't look me in the eye.

William appeared and sat down in the front next to Lila. I had never been in an intimate rehearsal with him, and the stakes felt high as if this one hour could determine the direction of my career.

Lila stopped the music and walked over to us. "You need to hold his arm with a stronger grip," she told me.

"Exactly, thank you," Jeff said to Lila, implying that I was making things difficult for him.

I was taken aback. If something didn't go well, would it always be my fault?

Lila moved on. "Jeff. Let's run your solo." She walked back to the front to restart the music. Did Lila agree that I should have this opportunity? Suddenly, I wasn't sure.

William crossed his arms and leaned back in his chair. His expression was cautiously optimistic.

The music began again, and Jeff danced his variation. I wiped sweat off my neck and tried to catch my breath. William nodded as Jeff finished with seven perfect *pirouettes* to the knee.

I ran into the center of the studio for my variation, determined to show William he hadn't made a mistake. The footwork in the choreography came naturally to me. Sweat ran into my eyes, and I danced the best I could.

At the end of my variation, I held the pose. Jeff began the finale section, the coda, as I walked to the side. William leaned forward, clasped his hands before him, and rested his elbows on his knees, fully engaged. My image in the mirror said it all: my face was red, I was soaked in sweat, and my hair was frizzy. I was desperate to please.

Jeff finished his leaps, and I came back on, nailing the *piqué* turns that traveled in a circle around the room. At the end of the phrase, Jeff ran back toward me for our final steps together. I had never practiced the final sequence with a partner, and the last shoulder sit didn't go well.

Our timing was off, and he couldn't lift me. We stumbled. I saw the angry look on his face. "Sorry," I managed. Lila shut the music off.

"Let's walk through this part," Lila said, waiting for us to recover.

Jeff walked in a circle and shook his legs.

"I can't believe this," he grumbled.

William stared out the window. Lila coaxed Jeff into marking the end again, and William stood and left the room.

The following day, I stood before the bulletin board and was surprised to see I had another *Spring Season* rehearsal with Jeff. After the first rehearsal, I thought they might take me out of it.

"Anna," Lila said behind me. I turned around and noticed we were alone in the hallway. "William wants you to dance *Spring Season* at a special gig in Park City, Utah next weekend."

"Me?"

"It's quite an honor that William wants to take you," she said, giving me a pointed look.

My mind was racing. Only principals did these side performances with William.

"Next weekend. You leave next Thursday. Nine days." She turned and hurried down the hall before I could say a word.

I had four *Spring Season* rehearsals the week before we left for the gig. Lila had to rehearse other ballets the company would perform in San Diego the following week, so Jeff and I were expected to run through things independently.

Jeff stood me up. I ended up using the studio time to practice by myself. He'd done the role many times before and didn't want to dance with a brand-new *corps de ballet* member.

Once, when I was little, my dad took me to his office and introduced me to all his work colleagues. "We've heard so much about you!" they said enthusiastically. "Your dad is very proud."

I turned red, flattered but scared at the same time. Why did they think they knew me so well, and what had Dad made me out to be?

William's plan to present me to the world wasn't any more apparent, but I knew I had to live up to something big.

CHAPTER 8

The airport bustled with activity on the day we left for Utah. We stood in the check-in line, William chatting with Natasha in front, Jeff, Adrienne, and Zif behind them discussing the altitude in Park City, Lorenzo stretching his calves, and Elizabeth filing her nails. When I saw them at work, they were the company's all-stars. I was struck by how comfortable they were with William and each other in a different setting.

"Are you excited?" Elizabeth asked me as we boarded the plane, and I nodded, unsure if she meant to be friendly or condescending. I sat quietly next to Adrienne and Zif on the flight. When we arrived, a shuttle service took us to the hotel.

"Meet in the lobby at seven," William said before we split up. "The party is at our sponsor's estate."

I was relieved to have some time alone in my hotel room. I had never had my own room on tour because the *corps* always had to double up. The mountain air was cold, and snow sparkled crystal clear outside my window.

Five minutes before seven, I walked into the lobby wearing an ankle-length strapless lavender sheath dress and high heels. Everyone had dressed as if we were going to the Academy Awards.

The eight of us climbed into a black stretch limousine outside the hotel, and the conversation floated around me as we drove. William wore an expensive-looking tuxedo and was in good spirits, smiling at everyone and relaxed in a way I'd never seen before. Natasha's cheeks flushed the same deep red as her dress as she laughed at something William said. Lorenzo loosened his tie and sat with his hips forward in the seat like a cologne ad. Even Jeff was in a good mood, exchanging dirty jokes with Lorenzo. Adrienne sat straight in a spaghetti-strap black evening dress and held Zif's hand while he whispered in her ear. Elizabeth stared out the window with an excited look on her face and whispered a few words to Adrienne. Her champagne-colored dress perfectly highlighted her delicate features.

We drove through a mountain pass. Finally, the limo pulled into a private driveway that wound through enormous trees. Eventually, the trees cleared away, and a mansion appeared.

"Wow," Adrienne said, speaking what everyone thought. We craned our necks to look out the window.

"That sure beats my lousy apartment," Jeff said.

Lorenzo slapped William's knee and said, "How about a raise?"

"I need one, too," William joked. "We'd better convince this sponsor to join the board."

An ice sculpture sparkled in the center of the circular driveway. Through the picture window, a grand piano stood in the living room, where people in gowns and tuxedos circulated. The scene took my breath away.

As we climbed out of the limo, the giant front doors opened toward us, and live jazz floated outside. We walked up the staircase toward an older woman in an emerald gown with matching evening gloves. She clasped her hands over the brilliant diamonds around her neck.

"The stars of the evening are here," she said joyously. "William, darling, it's been ages since you brought your kids. Come in." Her gloved hand beckoned to William as if they were old friends.

William joined her in the doorway and pecked her on the cheek. We each stopped to greet her. Adrienne hugged her, and Elizabeth and Natasha nodded politely. Much to her delight, Lorenzo, Zif, and Jeff graciously kissed her hand. As the other dancers entered the crowd, the hostess turned her attention to me.

"Who is this tiny young thing?" she asked William, smiling as she looked me over. "You didn't bring her the last time." She ran a gloved hand down his arm. I felt my face flush.

"What's your name, sweetheart?" she said. She looked from me to William and back. "You look like the Lilac Fairy with that snow glowing behind you."

"This is Anna Forester," William said, taking my arm and guiding me into the doorway. "She'll dance *Spring Season Pas de Deux* tomorrow, and she's one of my ones to watch."

"William!" she said. "You cast this child in your ballet? Well . . . isn't she just *ripe*? I don't think she even looks eighteen."

"I'm almost twenty," I said, and they chuckled.

"Well, that's almost old enough for a glass of wine," William said, taking my arm.

"Come," said the woman, and we followed her into the main room.

Natasha and Elizabeth were already in conversation with a group of male guests. Elizabeth looked surprisingly animated, and Natasha laughed flirtatiously at something a man in a tuxedo whispered to her. Natasha looked over when William walked in with me on his arm, and a noticeable flicker of jealousy crossed her face. Or maybe I'd imagined it?

A waiter in a tuxedo approached with a tray of white wine. "Chardonnay?" he asked.

"Thank you," William said, taking two glasses and handing one to me. "Let's toast," he said. "To your career. I have big plans for you."

I stared at him, dumbfounded. We clinked glasses.

"Now, hold it by the stem," he instructed me. "You don't want to warm the wine with your hand." He adjusted my glass accordingly.

A group of donors encircled us, and William introduced me around. Small talk dominated the evening, and by the time we left, my ears were full of which ballets the patrons liked and how excited they were that we were there.

I wasn't the only one anticipating my performance, which was a heady realization. William looked across the room at me with great pride. His content expression was one I would never forget, long after that night and even years after I left the company.

William gave class at the theater the following day. I felt intensely self-aware and glad that he couldn't overlook me. In a class of seven, there was nowhere to hide.

Partnering with Jeff could have been more comfortable during the dress rehearsal. He remained disconnected when we danced, and it was a miracle that we made it through the *pas de deux* without any significant mistakes. That was all I could realistically hope for without having rehearsed together.

There was a spread of sandwiches in the green room for us to eat between the rehearsal and the performance. Lorenzo and Zif put salami over their eyes and broccoli in their teeth and imitated the donors at last night's party. Adrienne, Natasha, and I laughed hysterically, and Jeff and Elizabeth looked on with more reserved amusement.

An hour before curtain, I started my makeup in the dressing room. I needed time to mentally prepare, and it was strange to share a dressing room next to the stage with Natasha, Adrienne, and Elizabeth. Usually, I was down in the theater basement with the *corps*, and people were always talking and goofing around. The principal dressing room was silent, and I wondered if it was always that way or if they weren't talking because of me.

Natasha cracked a few jokes, but Elizabeth and Adrienne said nothing. Elizabeth put on her headphones and went to work on her face. As I pinned in my headpiece, Adrienne stared at herself in the mirror, and Natasha sewed a pair of shoes.

For all the years I'd dreamed about reaching the top of my profession, sitting there, all I could see was how young and inexperienced I was compared with the seasoned principals.

The show began, and I dressed in my long blue romantic-style tutu and went to stage right to warm up. Zif danced *Muses* with Adrienne, Elizabeth, and Natasha. Every movement looked polished and infused with thought. They were sure of every step.

When *Muses* ended, I pulled my leg warmers off and jumped up and down to keep warm. Jeff walked into the back wing, and I followed him. There was only a pause in the program before *Spring Season Pas de Deux.*

"*Merde,*" I said. It was a critical moment, and I wanted to share it.

"*Merde,*" Jeff replied coldly. Our eyes met for the briefest second.

The curtain went up, and the music to *Spring Season* began. Jeff led me onto the stage and under the bright lights. There was scattered applause.

We began to dance. The smile on my face felt mechanical, but the steps ran smoothly. My confidence grew when I noticed that William wasn't scrutinizing me in the front wing, which meant he was sitting in the audience. I looked out at the dark house and let myself relax.

We reached the halfway point in the *adagio,* and out of nowhere, Jeff broke away from me and ran downstage right. This wasn't in the choreography.

He pantomimed a love gesture entirely off the music, kneeling to reach toward me. When he faced away from the audience, I saw a look of panic cross his face as he realized he had made a significant mistake. He had jumped ahead and blanked out sixteen counts in the choreography.

My familiar insecurities floated away in a sea of chaotic emotions. What a shocking, amateur mistake. He should have come to rehearsal. This would never have happened if we had practiced together.

I was tired of feeling inadequate. His eyes pleaded with me to go along. I would have to invent sixteen counts on the spot. My first performance of a principal role was supposed to go better, but this was it, and my next steps came naturally.

I smiled at the audience, and with a surprising burst of creativity, I improvised some *arabesques* and *piqué* turns. The look on Jeff's face as I danced toward him gave me confidence. He looked impressed. When I performed a brisk *soutenu* turn on the counts fifteen and sixteen, I was precisely on the music.

Jeff looked at me respectfully, a complete change from his earlier attitude. We picked up exactly as we should have within the original choreography. William was probably the only audience member who would know anything had gone wrong.

We finished the *adagio,* and I ran off so Jeff could begin his solo. Huffing and puffing, I tried to catch my breath.

Adrienne and Zif gave me an enthusiastic thumbs up from the wing across the stage.

I ran on for my variation, forgetting the studied angles of head and arms, painfully thought-out solitary rehearsals, and anger at Jeff. I performed on a new level. My dancing resonated with hard work. I didn't have to stay in line anymore, and I could just be myself all at once, dancing to my heart's content.

"Bravo!" someone yelled after my variation, and I grinned. There was nothing better than unbiased approval.

Jeff started the *coda*. I ran back onstage and whipped out my final sequence of turns. We confidently danced the ending together.

The stage went black, and Jeff lifted me from the final pose. When the lights came back on, he led me forward to bow, and no one unhooked my costume before the curtain fell because I wasn't even close to the back row of the *corps* anymore. All eyes were on me.

I extended my right arm over my head and slowly pointed my right foot behind me. My right hand came to my heart as I kneeled, bowing my head in a *grande révérance*. The applause rang as the audience rose to give us a standing ovation. When the curtain finally fell, I felt dizzy. I walked to the wing and sat down.

"Thank you," Jeff said quietly. I raised my head, and he smiled and looked me in the eye.

A warm hand rested on my shoulder. "How do you feel?" William asked, crouching down to look at my face.

"I feel great," I said.

William nodded. Standing back up, he turned to Jeff and said, "Good thing your partner can improvise."

Jeff cringed as William winked at me. Like a runner crossing the finish line, I closed my eyes and savored the victory.

A van dropped us back at the hotel after the show. Everyone was starving and tired.

"There's a brew pub across the street," William said as we climbed out of the van. "Let's celebrate."

We returned to the hotel after a meal filled with camaraderie I'd never seen within the larger company. William told inside jokes and made comments I didn't understand. They seemed to laugh at me initially, but I wasn't sure. I knew it was a privilege to be there, yet I couldn't have been more relieved when it was over.

Adrienne, Zif, Lorenzo, and Elizabeth got off the elevator a floor below Natasha, William, Jeff, and me. My room was the closest to the elevator, and I stopped to fumble for my key. Jeff paused two doors down on the other side as William and Natasha continued walking. Before entering my room, I glanced down the hall and saw William and Natasha laughing.

Jeff was still there, too, and he turned to look back at me. I snapped my mouth shut when our eyes met.

"Had enough?" he mouthed soundlessly.

"What do you mean?" I mouthed back.

He shook his head before he walked into his room.

My happiness over the performance evaporated, and I slammed the door as I walked into my room. The echo reverberated ominously down the hall. I sat on the bed. Why did I feel so lonely? I fell backward and stared at the ceiling.

I thought about a lot of things that night. It started to snow, and the flakes fell like a curtain outside my window. I thought of Karina's diary, which I hadn't picked up in weeks. There was so much she hinted at that I didn't understand. I thought of my parents, who had supported me my whole life to help me realize this dream, not knowing what it would be like. I thought of William and each principal and wondered about their lives. Who were they outside this strange ballet bubble?

On our first day back in L.A., Natasha and Elizabeth huddled in front of the bulletin board.

"What is this?" Elizabeth snapped, pointing at the schedule. "They only gave me one performance. She's in the *corps*."

I came around the corner, catching her comment and unsure what she meant. When I approached the board to check the schedule, Elizabeth glanced over her shoulder. "Oh!" she said sweetly. "Hi, Anna."

Natasha whipped her head around and stared at me.

Spring Season Pas de Deux had been added to the next program. Natasha and Jeff were the opening night cast, and Adrienne with Zif and Elizabeth with Lorenzo each had one scheduled performance. I was cast with Jeff to dance *Spring Season* six times in Los Angeles, Palm Springs, and San Diego. Even though I wasn't the first cast, I'd received far more performances than anyone else.

My parents flew in the day before I danced *Spring Season* in Los Angeles. Mom had come for one weekend the year before to see me in *Violins*, but Dad had never seen the company perform. They took a cab from the airport and settled in at my apartment before I came home from work.

I hobbled in the door at the end of the day and collapsed on the couch. The smell of dinner cooking filled the room. Mom walked out of the kitchen and regarded me.

"You look terrible," she said. She turned to look at Dad as he appeared behind her. "Look at the bags under her eyes. Anna, are you eating? There was no food in your fridge."

I didn't bother to tell her I'd been out of town. She didn't understand how hard it was to dance eight hours a day, every day. "Working hard, Mom. I've had no time to go the store."

"You have to take care of yourself," Dad said.

They were right, of course. I had noticed the bags under my eyes. My meals weren't consistently healthy, not on purpose, but because either I was on the road or didn't have time to shop and cook.

I barely had the energy to eat with them before I hit the bathtub and bed. It was hard for me to do everything myself. It wasn't true that dance was all I needed, even if that was the unspoken message surrounding me at work.

Something was missing, and my parents were a sharp reminder that what I needed, most of all, was love.

After opening night, my parents took me out to dinner.

After the food arrived, my mom said, "Guess what I heard the man next to me say when he saw your name in the program?"

"What?" I said, unsure what to expect but dreading anything that might contribute to the imposter syndrome I constantly felt at work.

Mom made a frustrated face. "He turned to his wife and said, 'That girl was just an apprentice last year. How did she get this big role? She must be sleeping with William.'"

I cringed, ashamed. I'd been working so diligently, trying to gain confidence in front of our local audience. Did they all see me as too inexperienced to legitimately earn my role?

"I almost leaned over and gave him a piece of my mind," Mom said, "but then I figured if he was going to say something else entertaining, I didn't want to stop him."

"Please tell me he made that comment before I danced," I said, looking at her pleadingly. I would never compromise myself for a role. My parents knew that.

"He did," said Mom, her face turning serious.

"Don't worry," Dad said. "He stood up and clapped enthusiastically with the rest of us."

CHAPTER 9

On my birthday, I danced my sixth and last performance of *Afternoon Symphony*. That night, Faye, Kelly, Ian, Mikey, and I celebrated at a neighborhood restaurant. We took a table in the back.

"Let me buy dessert," Ian announced. The waiter brought my favorite chocolate mousse cake. Ian said, "Happy Birthday, Golden Ticket."

I had been onstage nearly every night, either in the *corps de ballet* or as a principal, for the last three months. The stretch of nonstop performances had been the best time of my life. The frequency of being onstage made me more and more comfortable and confident with my job.

"Twenty must be your lucky age," Mikey said, smiling at me. He had become one of my biggest supporters once William singled me out. With many of the older dancers giving me the cold shoulder, I'd been incredibly grateful to him.

"Just be careful, my friend," Ian said, giving me an intense look. "The problem with William's golden ticket is that it expires."

I cringed, knowing how many dancers had come and gone. "I've heard."

"That's cynical," Faye said.

"They've worked you into the ground on a *corps* salary," Ian said. "All I'm saying is don't take it for granted. Someone else could be the new favorite next year."

"It's called paying my dues," I said, hurt.

Kelly cleared her throat. "I have something to tell everyone."

We turned our attention toward her.

"Miami offered me a contract," she said. "I'm leaving."

We had talked about other companies before; of course, we had, but I had thought they were abstract conversations. I had no idea Kelly was seriously considering leaving.

They hadn't cast her much again this season, but there were plenty of other people I'd thought were more likely candidates to jump ship.

"You're leaving?" Faye asked.

Kelly had been planning her departure for months if she had a contract lined up. She must have gone down to Miami to audition on a day off.

"I've done the roles I want to do in our repertory," Kelly said. "Miami is a great company, and I'm ready for a change. I'll be closer to my family in North Carolina, too."

I almost cried. I'd miss her. She seemed on the edge of a cliff, about to jump into a broader universe.

"Thanks," Kelly said, looking happier than I'd ever seen her. It occurred to me that her life in L.A. was as lonely as mine. She had lots of casual friends but wasn't particularly close to anyone. As far as I knew, her family never visited, and she didn't date. All the promotions in the world wouldn't change those aspects of her life.

While we discussed Kelly's plans for the move, I noticed Hilary and Ryan walk in and take a table near the front. They were holding hands.

We tried not to stare, but the drama was hard to ignore.

"Where's Rebecca?" Kelly asked.

"She was just talking this morning about a trip she and Ryan have planned," Mikey said.

Rebecca had no idea; we were sure of it. Seeing Ryan on a date with Hilary was a shock.

It had been a strange couple of weeks, full of little things that at the time seemed insignificant, facial expressions and comments whispered in the hallway, all blurred together—in hindsight, the moments rearranged themselves in my mind to form a pattern that had been there for months. Hilary near Rebecca in the dressing room while Rebecca complained about Ryan's inattentiveness. Ryan and Hilary flirting by the vending machine. Rebecca's forlorn expression while she watched Ryan dance.

The conversation moved on and shifted to lighter topics, but the question was still on everyone's mind. After a few minutes, Hilary put her hand on Ryan's knee.

By then, I was ready to go. We paid our bill and left the restaurant, pretending not to see them as we passed by.

"I hope that isn't going where I think it's going," Kelly said as we parted ways. "I'm going to give Rebecca a call."

"I hope she's OK," I said.

The guys I used to dream about were self-centered and charming, like Ryan. They bored quickly and took their attractiveness for granted. But someone who appreciated me and had my back was a different thing, one I couldn't imagine finding in my present life, not how I was shut off from the outside world.

For the first time, I thought about Ethan and how rude I'd been to him when he clobbered me with the tree branch. He'd left me that nice note backstage and I'd trashed it.

I hoped Hilary could handle how much Elizabeth's friends would hate her when they found out. That rush of feeling when Ryan kissed her, or that crackle of electricity in her fingertips when he touched her hand, better be worth it.

I couldn't imagine what Hilary felt with Ryan was the power of being truly loved. But I could understand her being lonely. Maybe she needed to pretend.

My contract came in the mail a few days later. Secretly, I'd hoped for a promotion. It was early; I had only technically been in the *corps* for one year, but Kelly and several other dancers were leaving, and there was an opening for a new soloist.

The letter invited me back as a second-year *corps* member with a raise of twenty dollars a week. I rationalized the reasons. The company had financial problems. William thought I was too young.

I called Faye. "Second-year *corps* for me, too," she said. "No one got promoted. William spent the budget on next year's premiere of *America*."

America was a Roizman classic and a massive production for a company of our size. We were not Ballet New York with ninety dancers. We had forty-five, which meant every dancer in the company would be in the ballet without a second cast.

"He's trying to hire some Canadian superstar next year," Faye said. "Grant something-or-other. Supposedly, *America* is the lure." That made sense. The *pas de deux* in *America* was a showstopper.

I jogged around the stage in Palm Springs at the ten-minute call for the last show of the season. I knew I should have been thinking about the choreography, but instead, I was thinking about why I didn't have a boyfriend. Was something wrong with me?

That night, I was in the *corps* of *Pathways*, one of the most challenging ballets in the repertory because there were no exits, and the steps required tremendous stamina. I had only danced it twice. Ian was my partner, and even though he was my friend, I dreaded dancing with him. I came away with bruises every time we ran the ballet. The worst part was his attitude. I had repeatedly asked him not to dig his fingers into my ribs, and he rolled his eyes and joked about it.

I wondered what it would be like to work in a situation where I wore regular clothes and didn't have to let someone touch me if I didn't want them to. We were all so familiar with each other. If I complained, people would think I was challenging to work with.

"Five minutes," said the new stage manager. "Five minutes, please." I glanced at him as I walked to my starting spot on the stage. The way Greg's replacement didn't make eye contact made me feel like he didn't see us. Greg had recently left the company for a new job, and I missed his reassuring presence.

"I want Greg back," Ian said, echoing my thoughts. "I don't think this new stage manager knows what he's doing."

We relied heavily on the stage manager for *Pathways* because the ballet didn't have an overture. Backstage, the only warning that the performance was about to start was when the stage manager called "places." The audience applauded the silence when the curtain went up, giving the impression that the applause made the ballet begin.

Ian got down on the floor to do push-ups, and I faced the curtain and did *relevés*. Ryan boxed air, Allison tried a *pirouette*, and Mikey jumped up and down. Rebecca was down on the floor in the splits, glaring at Ryan's back.

"I can't believe this is the last show," Rebecca told Mikey. "I'm so ready for vacation."

She had been a shadow of herself. A week ago, Rebecca and Hilary had gotten into a screaming match in the dressing room, and since then, they had kept their distance. Ryan had been trying to break it off with Hilary since. He no longer seemed to think she was worth the drama. How could they have assumed the affair would be private when we were all in each other's business?

When the curtain unexpectedly rose, Lorenzo was in the middle of practicing a lift with Elizabeth. I don't think we truly believed it was happening. For all the time I spent worrying about messing up onstage, I'd never contemplated the possibility of a problem so entirely out of my control.

Only the luckiest dancers make it through their careers without at least one significant embarrassment onstage. While I expected my moment of shame would happen eventually, I never thought it would be as random as the curtain rising at the wrong time. I'd always assumed a public humiliation would be my fault.

Rebecca uttered a string of curse words and jumped off the floor.

"Why didn't he call places?" Mikey hissed.

Elizabeth and Lorenzo ran offstage. I hopped to my opening pose, horror rising inside of me. The audience laughed.

Our new stage manager had ruined the entire ballet.

The music began. I performed the first combination but was so shaken up that I could hardly remember the choreography. My body knew exactly what to do from muscle memory, which saved me since my mind was elsewhere. I stepped on something and stumbled.

"Watch it, Anna," Ian said from down on the floor. He hadn't noticed the rising curtain and was still mid-push-up. Out of the corner of my eye, I saw him slowly turn his head to the side and look where he thought the curtain should be.

"What the—?" he said. The audience roared at the look of utter bewilderment on Ian's face. He lost his temper fast and hissed, "I'm going to kill someone."

I fought the urge to laugh. Ian sprung to his feet, grabbed my hands, and picked up the choreography. The ballet continued, and every time he touched me, I could feel his anger.

At the end, the audience applauded, and we took our bows. When the curtain fell, I looked down at my wrists and noticed the purple and yellow bruises already forming where Ian had grabbed me. My ribs throbbed.

"Look what you did," I accused. I pushed my arm in front of his face.

Ian gave me a wide-eyed look of surprise. "Did I do that?" he asked, genuinely confused.

"Yes," I said, exasperated. I didn't have the energy to push the issue.

The new stage manager approached us. "Sorry, guys," he said sheepishly. "I forgot to call places."

Didn't he know our professional reputation was at stake every time the curtain rose?

"They better fire you," Ian said bitterly.

The stage manager stared at us stupidly. Disgusted, I turned away and followed Allison and Rebecca offstage.

Rebecca said, "This was one for the books."

Elizabeth was sobbing by the prop table. She was the principal, and the audience would remember her in conjunction with the incident more than any of us in the *corps*. Lorenzo was a few feet away, kicking the wall in frustration.

William appeared. "Where's that idiot?" he roared. "He's dead!" He marched over to the stage manager, shouting. I hurried to the dressing room, eager to leave the mess behind.

With that, my second season was over.

CHAPTER 10

We returned to work in June with four new apprentices, three girls and one boy. They seemed so young. I missed Kelly. Across the room, I noticed there was one more new dancer.

He looked too confident to be an apprentice and had a handsome face, dark hair, and a compact, muscular body. His nose was sunburned.

Standing at his usual barre spot, Mikey followed my gaze.

"That's Grant," Mikey whispered. "The new Canadian principal. He's only twenty-four. Do we need a new leading man?"

Mikey sucked in his gut and studied himself in the mirror. I glanced at him and noticed he had put on weight. His hair wasn't washed.

"He's handsome," I said. "I wonder who they'll pair him with. Natasha?"

"He's too short to partner with any of the principals," Mikey said.

Grant quickly established his position amid company politics. He remained reserved with the dancers and overly ingratiating with the staff. We watched jealously as William joked around with him during class.

The men disliked Grant even more because the girls appreciated his good looks. He whipped off eight beautiful *pirouettes* and sliced through the air, inspiring awe—and resentment.

I worked diligently during the rehearsal period. In addition to all the new *corps* roles in Roizman ballets, I learned one of the principals in *Afternoon in the Park* and a soloist role in *Tidal Moods*.

"William and Lila took Grant to dinner?" Allison asked Rebecca in the dressing room. "What's up with that?"

Rebecca studied herself in the mirror. "They'll do anything to make sure he stays. Maybe they're worried he's lonely."

"He looks lost in rehearsal," Allison said. "He's never danced a Roizman ballet in his life."

I peeled off my tights and said, "He doesn't have any friends, especially if he's spending his free time with the artistic staff."

Allison popped her gum. "Elizabeth is supposed to dance the premiere of *America* with him, and she's not happy. He's too short for her."

The big focus of the summer rehearsal season was *America*, which would premiere six months later in January. One of the official people from the Roizman Foundation came in from New York to set *America* for us, and William hired several local ballet students to understudy the *corps*.

America was the only ballet in our repertory that simultaneously used every dancer in the company. The casting was a logistics nightmare.

The premiere of *America* would be an enormous achievement for a company of our size. If we pulled it off well, the dance community and the city of Los Angeles would regard us with new respect.

The fall season opened in Los Angeles, and I danced more than almost anyone else in the *corps de ballet* every night. It was an honor to be cast so frequently, and it reassured me my career was going well. The downside was I was always tired and had no life outside of work.

"Anyone want to go out for dinner before the performance tonight?" Hilary asked unexpectedly in the dressing room.

I was cleaning out my theater case and kept my head down as people made excuses.

The room cleared, and Hilary sat on the bench beside me.

"The Ryan thing was over months ago," she said. "When are people going to get over it? He used *me*."

Ryan had been trying to get Rebecca back. I felt sorry for her. People weren't going to forget. We watched the drama every hour of the workday.

In early November, I rehearsed lead Marzipan in *Nutcracker*. It was my third year performing the ballet, and I had officially earned my way out of the lowest *corps* roles. I wondered how long it would take to graduate from Grandma.

At the end of a run of shows in Palm Springs, I drove home late after dancing in all three ballets on the program. Faye caught a ride back with me, and I was so tired I worried I might drive off the road.

"Talk to me so I stay awake," I said as I pressed down on the gas. All I wanted was to get home and go to bed.

"I don't have much to say," Faye said sadly. She hadn't been cast much. There didn't seem to be much life to her dancing lately. "I wish I was onstage more. I talked to Lila last week, and she said to keep working hard and not get injured. That was it."

"She didn't give you any reason for how little they're using you?"

"If they don't say anything specific, they don't have to make promises they won't keep," she said sadly.

"*Merde,* Anna," said Kirsten, one of the new apprentices, before I went on for my first performance of lead Marzipan in *Nutcracker.* She was one of the four *corps de ballet* girls who danced behind me, a significant opportunity for her first year.

"Is this your first Marzipan?" I asked.

She smoothed down her tutu. "Yes," she said, biting her lip.

"*Merde* to you too." I squeezed her hands.

The music began, and I led the *corps* girls onstage. I noticed Grant in the front wing right behind William. The orchestra sounded beautiful, and I put extra emphasis on my musicality. Finishing the variation, I hit a perfect quadruple step-up turn and even stayed on pointe at the end, perfectly on balance, kneeling precisely on the last note. The audience applauded enthusiastically, along with everyone backstage.

"Great job," Faye said, giving me a high-five when I hit the wing before she ran on for Waltz of the Flowers. I grabbed some water from the cooler and watched Natasha as the Dewdrop.

Faye finished and came to sit next to me backstage. While we waited for the finale, we both sat transfixed, watching Adrienne and Zif dance the Sugar Plum Fairy's *pas de deux.*

Nutcracker season raced by, and in no time, it was January, and we were back to company class and rehearsal. I put my bag at my usual barre spot across from Mikey.

"Welcome back, Golden Ticket," Ian said as he walked past me. "It looks like you hit the jackpot for the winter run."

I had so little patience for his teasing. "What does that mean?"

Faye looked up from tying her pointe shoes. "Congratulations."

I looked at her inquisitively.

"Did you see the board?" Faye asked.

"No. I don't even know today's schedule."

Mikey snorted. "You should take a look," he said.

I walked out into the hall. Allison, Natasha, and Jeff stood clustered around the board.

"What the hell?" Allison said, pointing at today's schedule, her back to me. I had a strong feeling of *déjà vu*.

"Grant asked for her," Jeff told Natasha.

"This is insanity," Allison said, and it felt just like when the *Spring Season* casting went up. "Why is he replacing Elizabeth?" she continued. "Has she seen this yet?"

"Elizabeth is at physical therapy," Natasha said. "But she's fine. The premiere is next week."

I asked, "What's going on?"

Allison, Elizabeth, and Jeff jumped at the sound of my voice.

"See for yourself," Allison said. Natasha backed away, and Jeff gestured toward the board. I stepped closer and saw that my first rehearsal of the year was for the *America pas de deux* with Grant.

I sat down on a bench and tried to process the news. "What's going on with Elizabeth?"

"Does it matter to you?" Allison snapped. I looked up at her, taken aback. She turned away and stomped into the studio.

William could have let me rehearse the *America* principal last summer if he had seen me in the role. This kind of thing never happened. Why did all the principals receive plenty of time to prepare, yet if they put me onstage, they gave me only a week's notice?

Class began, and I went through the motions, my mind elsewhere. I wondered if William would say something, but he hardly looked at me. Was this a test? I was just a twenty-year-old third-year *corps de ballet* dancer. This was different from *Spring Season Pas de Deux*. The entire company would dance behind me in *America*.

Why would William cast me as Grant's partner? The reputation of Los Angeles Ballet Theater would rest on my shoulders. It had to be just a rehearsal, not a casting decision. They must have decided I should understudy the role.

Once I settled on the idea that I was an understudy, I found it easier to concentrate on class. People were jumping to too many conclusions. What was wrong with Elizabeth, anyway?

After class, I met Grant in the small studio. We exchanged a friendly smile and resumed business, stretching and examining ourselves in the mirror.

"Do you know what's wrong with Elizabeth?" I asked him.

"Nothing is wrong with her," he said. "I asked to dance with you."

Lila arrived, looking tan and rested after our week off. "Let's get started," she said. "We don't have a lot of time."

I wondered if she'd played a role in calling me to the rehearsal. Lila seemed less of an ally when William singled me out. This role was too important to come from anyone but William.

She talked us through the choreography, and Grant took my hand to mark together. I had watched the *America pas de deux* a few times. I always danced in the *corps de ballet* in rehearsals, so if I did the lead, who would dance my *corps* part? The cast used up the entire company. They would have to hire someone from the school to do my *corps* part. I must be an understudy only.

Lila indicated the final lift and said, "OK, Anna. That's the *adagio*. We'll work on your variation, the coda, and the opening and finale later. William should be here in a minute."

Ten minutes to learn it before I danced in front of him. "OK." I frantically reviewed the sequence, and Grant marked behind me, confident and professional.

William strode into the studio and leaned on the barre, looking energized in a crisp pink button-down shirt and black pants. "How's it going?" he asked casually.

"Good," Lila said. Grant and I continued to mark the steps.

"Let's see what we have," William said. He walked over to stand by Lila in the front of the room.

Lila hit play, and Grant and I danced the first thirty-two counts of the *adagio*. Grant was a good partner, and I did my best to match his competence. My arms shook when he walked me in a circle on pointe in *arabesque*. The partnering was complicated, and I was aware of my lack of experience. Elizabeth could have done the choreography in her sleep.

"Stop," William said. "Let me show you." Lila switched off the music. I wiped the sweat off my forehead. Grant stepped to the side so William could take my hand.

"Hold your back," William commanded. He gently brushed my scapula with his free hand to indicate which muscles he wanted me to engage.

"Lock your arm in place," he said. We danced the first few steps. His touch was expert. "You try," William said to Grant. He stepped away from me but hovered to make sure Grant mimicked him. Lila watched intently from the front.

I took Grant's hand, and we began again, still tentative at certain parts in the choreography. We made it through the beginning.

"Stop," William said. He walked back and took hold of me to advise Grant. I examined my reflection in the mirror. A tiny girl, only five-foot-three and ninety-eight pounds, looked back. On my right was a living legend; on my left, a younger version. What was I doing there?

Grant and I danced the *adagio* several times and grew more comfortable. The experience of dancing with someone who wanted to partner with me was a world away from Jeff.

By the end, we were exhausted. I could do the steps, but could I make them look as good as Elizabeth or Adrienne?

I thanked all three of them, and William touched my shoulder. "You have a lot of work to do," William said. "Your back is too weak. Do push-ups every morning. Grant can't partner you if you can't hold yourself up."

"I will," I said, nodding emphatically.

William nodded, satisfied, and walked out of the studio. Grant reached over and took my hand. He squeezed my fingers reassuringly.

I hobbled home every day that week during my lunch hour and sat in the bathtub. My muscles burned. I felt out of shape, and the choreography in the *pas de deux* was different from anything I had ever danced. I rehearsed with Grant for two hours every day after morning class, and in the afternoon, I rehearsed my *corps* part. The artistic staff's casting intentions still weren't clear.

On my way to the afternoon rehearsal on Friday, I looked at the board and saw the casting for the opening weekend had been posted. My name was next to Grant's for opening night. I would dance the principal role in the premiere the following Thursday. That meant I had six days to become a star.

The company had settled into a common belief that I was learning *America* just for rehearsal and that Elizabeth would dance the performances. It seemed impossible William would put me onstage in such a prominent role.

My life had become a story that only happened in ballet movies like *The Turning Point* and *Center Stage*. There was no reason for this casting drama. We had enough principals to dance *America* on opening night with Grant, even if he didn't want to dance with Elizabeth. What about Natasha? Couldn't Adrienne dance with Grant? Or even a soloist or senior *corps* member who had been been in the company much longer than me?

Traditionally, the younger *corps* members on a promotion track spent years dancing their leading roles at the Sunday matinee. It took years to become the marquee star of the company. So why was this happening to me, and why this way? People were jealous, and the sad part was that I was having difficulty being happy. The pressure felt like a noose around my neck. What if I let everyone down?

The entire company assembled in the big studio. Lila looked stressed out. Since we'd worked on the ballet last summer, this afternoon was the first time all the sections would come together. William arrived, and the dancers cleared out of his way as he cut across the floor to join Lila.

"Let's face away from the mirror," Lila said. She put her chair in the middle of the window in front of the Third Street Promenade and gave us an authentic audience: the pedestrians. Opening night was only a day away.

A ballet about to premiere was like a meal about to be eaten: the hard work and dirty dishes abandoned in the kitchen, the food about to disappear fast, but the moment when the people sat down to feast made it all worth it. William looked like he was about to eat at the finest restaurant in L.A. Pedestrians gathered outside the window at the sight of all the activity.

Lorenzo, leaning against a barre on the side, noticeably flinched. I followed his eyes to the doorway. Elizabeth stood there dressed in street clothes. She walked in and sat in a plastic chair in the corner. Allison hurried over to her, and they started whispering. Elizabeth looked pale and tired. I'd barely seen her since all of this began, and the idea of her watching me dance her role unnerved me.

"Places," Lila called. Fifteen girls formed a triangle in the center of the floor, and the music began. I stretched on the side of the room and watched the girl they had hired from the school rehearse my part in the *corps*. She had been understudying several *corps* spots since last summer, and this was a great opportunity for her.

A group of fifteen girls danced the second movement, and while they twirled, I stood up and practiced a few little jumps. Adrienne walked over to me carrying a practice tutu.

"Wear this," Adrienne whispered kindly. She helped me put the tutu on.

Fifteen boys danced the third movement, showing their high jumps and turns. William watched intently, and Lila wrote down corrections to save for the end. Grant winked at me across the room. Despite the pressure, I liked working with him.

My opinion of Grant had changed since we'd been rehearsing. The more I knew him, the less arrogant he seemed, at least when we were alone. In company class, he still paraded around like he was king of the world. I realized his behavior came from insecurity rather than egotism. Maybe all of us were lonelier than I realized.

The music to the *pas de deux* began, and Grant stepped onto the floor. I walked on four counts later, he offered me his hand, and I placed mine in his. We made eye contact, and then I looked out, took in my audience, and realized I had never been so terrified.

Dozens of my peers and closest friends stood or sat on the floor next to Lila and William. Behind them, a crowd of strangers, through the window, eyed me expectantly.

I stepped onto pointe and took Grant's hand for the *promenade,* but emotions poured over me. Something inside me lurched. I should have danced my best, but instead, I fell flat on my face.

I lay there face down, momentarily in shock, while Lila stopped the music. The room went dead silent. Grant helped me slowly stand up. Tears pooled in my eyes, and I bit my lip to prevent them from coming.

I'd had one of the most stressful weeks of my life. But an audience doesn't pay a hundred dollars a ticket to hear excuses.

William took my arm gently, pulling me away from Grant. I felt Elizabeth's eyes boring into my back. They were all staring at me.

"If you're not ready, you don't have to do this," William said quietly. Our eyes met, and even if he intended to be kind, all I saw in his expression was a challenge. I looked away from William and caught the determined expression on Grant's face.

"I can do it," I insisted, locking eyes with William again. This was what my entire life had been leading up to. How could I not be ready?

People began to whisper, and William nodded after a moment of consideration. Grant pumped his fist.

"Let's try that again," William said. He went back to his seat. I rolled my neck a few times, took a deep breath, and walked over to the side of the room. I was my own best coach, telling myself I could do it. No one was coming to do this for me. I was the one. This was on my shoulders.

The music to the *pas de deux* began, and Grant stepped onto the floor. I walked on four counts later, he offered me his hand, and I placed mine in his. When I felt his grip, solid and sure, our bodies connected in a way they hadn't before. I could feel the heat coming off him; our shared determination felt like a new power. The renewed energy made the fall seem less critical, like a dream, and the world of the ballet became our reality. We smiled at each other as I stepped on pointe.

We danced the entire *adagio,* and Grant flew through his variation. I made it through my solo without mistakes. The coda sped by, and as we neared the end, the other dancers walked to the side to get in place for the finale. Forty people posed around us in formation when Grant and I came back center stage. We danced alone again briefly before the whole company joined in behind us. As the finale ended, Grant lifted me on his shoulder. I saluted on the last note.

Lila stopped the music. "Good. Let's talk about the first movement," she said. The girls crowded around her, and Grant and I moved over to the side of the room. We were both out of breath and exchanged a look of commiseration.

"Not bad," he said, squeezing my shoulder.

I said, "Sorry, I was so nervous."

"Don't worry," he said. "We dance well together."

William coached Jeff on his turns. While we waited for feedback, I turned to face the mirror and practiced some *pirouettes.*

"Let's talk about your variation," William said to Grant, beckoning to him. I stopped practicing to watch as they walked through a few steps. I leaned on the barre and admired Grant mirroring William's *port de bras.*

Dancers began to filter out of the room. William indicated that Grant should demonstrate. Grant launched into the air and bent his knees above his waist, executing a spectacular jump.

"Good," William said, rubbing his hands together. "We'll keep working on it, guys. Keep building your arm strength, Anna." He turned to me and nodded approvingly.

"I will." The three of us smiled at each other. I felt a glimmer of excitement.

I walked past Elizabeth on my way out, wondering if I should apologize to her. She touched my wrist. "Congratulations," she said. Her eyes looked sad, but she gave me a smile.

CHAPTER 11

At four in the afternoon on the premiere day, I tied my sneakers in the dressing room. The tech rehearsal was over, and I had to return by seven-thirty for the half-hour call. The *America pas de deux* was at the end of the program and wouldn't start until ten. Everyone else had already left, and I was starving. The door to the dressing room opened, and I couldn't believe my eyes when I saw who walked in.

"Jen?"

My old roommate from SBNY threw her arms around me and shouted, "Surprise!"

Jen was so busy with her career in New York that I couldn't imagine how she got away. My eyes filled with tears.

Back in high school, she was the one I cried with after terrible classes, laughed with after seeing a good Broadway show, and turned to for help after I fainted in my workshop performance. Jen was there for every big moment I had in New York, so it was fitting she would be there to see the most important performance of my professional career.

"You didn't think I would miss this milestone, did you?" she asked.

We hugged and jumped up and down like little kids. I packed up quickly so we could go out to eat, renewed by the reassurance that our friendship had stood the test of time and distance.

After dinner, I made sure Jen had a ticket. She sat backstage with me while I did my hair and makeup, and then I sent her out front to enjoy the show. I watched the opening ballet from the wings while I warmed up.

At intermission, I returned to the dressing room to put on my costume and found two bouquets on my chair. My parents had sent sunflowers, and Grant sent roses. A card was on top of my makeup case from all the girls in the *corps de ballet.*

A dresser fastened me into my blue and gold costume. I tied my pointe shoes, applied red lipstick, and headed for the stage. I was ready to live out every little girl's dream.

Grant met me onstage at the five-minute call and kissed my cheek. I could tell he was excited.

"Thank you for the flowers," I said as he took both of my hands in his own.

"Of course," he said enthusiastically. "We're going to be great." He led me to the front of the stage to practice the lifts that gave us trouble in rehearsal.

"Places," the new stage manager called a few minutes later. Grant caught me off-guard by pecking me on the lips. I was too dumbfounded to say anything. We separated and walked to opposite sides of the stage. I didn't see William, so I assumed he was in the audience. The fifteen *corps* girls took their places, and everything went black.

There was applause as the overture began, and I could feel the energy in the theater. More applause poured out of the house as the curtain rose. The girls grinned as they moved through their formations. I wondered if Elizabeth was in the audience.

The second group of girls took the stage, kicking their legs to their ears. Time flew by. When the men went on, I started to jog in place.

"*Merde*," people whispered as they passed me. I stepped into the back wing, and the music to the *pas de deux* began.

Grant stepped onstage, and I followed four counts later. He offered me his hand, and I put mine in his, feeling his energy like a jolt of electricity. We smiled and danced together in a concentrated effort. My whole body grew warm underneath the spotlight as we performed the *adagio*. Our performance was flawless, except for a tiny fumble during the partnered turns right at the end. It was a small error I could live with.

"Perfect," Grant whispered. We walked forward to bow. I exited the stage, and he launched into his variation. I tried to regain my breath. The audience applauded when I ran on for my solo. I jumped, whirled, and became the music. It was fun.

"Yes!" I told myself as I whipped out a series of double turns, perfectly on my leg. By the end of the section, I was so tired that I couldn't feel my muscles. Somehow, I managed to bow and run off.

Grant tore through the air as the coda began. I ran on for a series of consecutive turns on one leg, and he saluted while I was already in motion. After a double *pirouette* at the end of the *fouettés*, I marched around on *pointe*, hit the wing, and posed with one leg in *arabesque*, holding my balance far into the following musical phrase. The audience clapped and whistled. While Grant flew around the stage, I ran to the back wing.

"Go, Anna!" Faye cheered.

I re-entered, spinning across the stage as Grant stepped in to partner me. He tossed me high and sweat flew off us like a sprinkler. The music to the *pas de deux* ended with a joyous crescendo as we ran into the wings.

"We're almost done," Grant whispered, pumping his fist victoriously. "We nailed it."

I squeezed his shoulder, too tired and out of breath to manage anything but a grin.

The *corps* danced the opening to the finale and then posed as Grant and I ran back under the lights. The entire company danced together as the ballet came to an end. Grant lifted me on his shoulder, and I saluted on the last note. The curtain fell.

Grant lowered me to the ground. I took his hand. We bowed as the curtain flew up and then back down. Everyone raced for the wings except the first fifteen girls, who hurried to line up. My face glowed with pride as I watched the rest of the company take their bows.

Grant stepped onstage and offered me his hand. He led me to the center in front of the cast, and we walked forward to the stage's apron. I extended my right arm over my head and pointed my right foot behind me. My right hand came to my heart as I kneeled and bowed in a *grande révérance.*

The audience stood up to applaud. I ran to the front wing and led the conductor out onstage. "You were beautiful," the *maestro* said. I squeezed his hand.

A board member in a tuxedo presented me with a massive bouquet of red, white, and blue flowers, and I pulled out a red rose and presented it to Grant.

"Bravo!" the audience shouted.

Our fingers touched as Grant accepted the rose. He dropped to his knee to kiss my hand as the curtain fell.

"You were wonderful," he said, looking into my eyes. We were both so happy.

Dancers exited into the wings, pulling pins out of their hair and tugging at their costumes. I stood at the front of the stage, my arms filled with flowers, inhaling the sweat mixed with roses and rosin.

Lila walked past, her short hair whipping her in the face as she turned to look back at me. "It went well except for the end of the *adagio*," she said curtly. "Good job."

William walked over to kiss my cheek and shake Grant's hand. He rested his hand on my shoulder, and his rare smile told me he was pleased.

People patted me on the back and congratulated me as I walked off the stage, eager to collapse, remove my makeup, and take a long, hot shower.

"Wait," Grant said behind me. He took my arm and steered me into a dark corner.

"Is everything OK?" I asked. Before the words were out, Grant kissed me. Maybe it was the excitement of the evening or the sheer physicality of our dance connection, but for a split second, I couldn't help myself and kissed him back. He grabbed my shoulders and pulled me closer.

But here's the thing. The ballet part of me *was* caught up in all of it. Overwhelmed. I'd been alone for so long. I'd been lonely for so long. Grant was handsome and kind and a good partner. But I didn't know anything about who he was outside the studio. And when he kissed me, I realized that whatever it was that I needed was far, far away from the stage. I thought of Ethan, someone I hardly knew and hadn't seen in two years.

As always, my professional life interrupted my personal one. "Congratulations, Anna!" called one of the prominent donors, and I left Grant and went to talk to her. She kissed me on the cheek and introduced me to her friends. I hugged her and put on my best stage smile. When she let me go, I headed straight for the dressing room.

Jen read me the reviews over breakfast the following day. "The premiere of *America* is a stunning achievement for William Mason and the Los Angeles Ballet Theater. Mason's choice to cast a young *corps* dancer in the ballerina role was a pleasant surprise. Anna Forester faced the technical demands of the *pas de deux* with charm and ease. It's a role she can certainly grow into . . ."

"What a relief," I said, sipping hot coffee.

Jen said, "This is going to make your whole career."

"Why do I feel so confused?" I asked. "What should I say to Grant?"

"Anyone would have been caught up considering the situation," Jen said. "I say go for it."

After I dropped Jen at the airport, I went to work. Grant caught my eye and winked in company class, and much to my chagrin, I realized I kept looking at him. Afterward, he caught up to me in the hallway as I went to the dressing room.

"Want to get some lunch after the next rehearsal? I'm done at one," he said.

"Oh, I can't, I'm too busy," I said awkwardly.

"We need to talk."

"I know," I said with a sigh.

"I want to get to know you better. We have a good thing going here." It wasn't what I had expected. I had thought Grant was playing around.

"Grant, I love dancing with you, but I don't want to date someone in the company," I said.

"Don't you?" he asked. "You're the biggest bunhead here. I know how you kissed me, and what do you have in common with a non-dancer anyway? Work it out for yourself. You'll come around." He kissed my lips firmly and returned to rehearsal, leaving me more confused than ever.

Grant was confident he wouldn't have to wait long for me, and he was right about one thing: I had kissed him back and enjoyed it. But he represented something I didn't want or need more of. I loved ballet, and it was a massive part of me. But it was too much.

I wanted a person who loved me not because I was a dancer but despite it.

The season ended quietly. After the *America* run, I went back to dancing in the *corps*. There were no casting surprises, and as much as I hoped I'd get more solos, *America* seemed to be my big moment of the year. I could live with it.

When our contracts came in the mail, I didn't get promoted. I had expected to become a soloist, even though I knew I was young and hadn't been in the company as long as many other *corps* girls. After *America*, I felt I deserved it.

I tried to convince myself that William had a plan for me, as he had promised. I swallowed my pride and jumped back into work, convinced I would work harder than ever and receive more opportunities next year. Eventually, he had to promote me if he continued to use me as a principal. Didn't he?

CHAPTER 12

My career turned downward on the first day of my fourth season. I looked at the rehearsal schedule and saw that Hilary had been called to learn the lead in *Fire*. I was only called to rehearsals for the *corps*.

"What is going on?" Faye whispered to me in the back of the studio while the first group executed the *pirouette* combination. "Why is Hilary, of all people, learning *Fire*? Why not you? You were great in *America*."

"Maybe I did something wrong," I said.

Faye shook her head. "Ballet politics make me crazy."

William looked right through me.

I picked up Karina's diary that night. I'd forgotten about it for a long time.

William has a new favorite, Teresa. She's only been in the company two years and is all of twenty. I wish we knew what he saw in her. Her face is pretty, but her feet and extension aren't that great, and her technique is sloppy. It's hard watching her get the opportunities many older girls in the corps deserve instead. Allison has been here five years already, and she's furious. She was so ready to vent that she didn't even come up for air when we spoke.

Allison: "I'd like to ask William what he sees in Teresa and why he plays favorites for a season but doesn't stay loyal to people year after year. He's a father figure to us, and this company is one big dysfunctional family. Why does management treat us like children? We're grown adults.

All I've ever wanted is to be a dancer, so it feels like a big screw-you when he casts these fresh-faced kids right out of ballet school into the significant roles I've been passed over for. I take his decisions personally.

I've been frustrated throughout my career. It's a struggle because I feel so lucky to have my job and dance with such a great company. So many kids never realize this dream. It's problematic that the man who gave me this incredible opportunity is the same one who regularly breaks my heart."

I read Allison's passage in Karina's diary several times. If that was how Allison felt back when the journal was written, I can only imagine what she thought of me when I was dancing *America.* It must be so hard to spend ten years in the *corps,* watching the cycle of newcomers have their moment. How many of William's favorites became principals? Not many. I had never even heard of Teresa. What happened to her?

Elizabeth and Lorenzo went first at the full company rehearsal of *Fire*. There was time for a second run-through, and Lila told Hilary to dance the lead. After my *corps* part, I sat on the side and watched Hilary and Grant dance the *pas de deux*.

I was jealous that she was dancing with him. I had been careful to avoid him since the new season started, and I'd heard he was dating someone. I didn't miss Grant; it was the feeling of being special enough to be his partner. Dancing with him once I had found my confidence was *fun*.

Lila peppered them with compliments. I wondered if she noticed how much I was glaring at her. The more I watched them, the more I wanted to quit. Eventually, I couldn't take it anymore and went into the hallway to get some air.

"Hey, Ian," I said, sitting beside him on the bench. He seemed bored. I watched him chug a soda in one gulp.

"Hi, princess," he said. "How's it going?"

"Oh, fine, I guess."

"I thought you'd be learning *Fire*," he said. "I guess Hilary is the new golden ticket."

"Don't get me started."

He patted my knee. "Sorry, Forester."

"Ian," I said, "do you know anything about a former dancer in the company named Teresa?"

Adrienne and Zif were sitting on a nearby couch and sharing a sandwich. They immediately looked over.

"Teresa?" Adrienne echoed.

"Where did you hear about her?" Zif asked.

"Oh geez," Ian said. He sighed.

"I don't know," I said, "I just heard she was William's favorite a few years back and wondered what happened to her. Did she get promoted? Did she go to another company?"

"No, and no," Adrienne said.

I stood up and faced them. "Did she quit?"

"She quit, alright," Ian said. "But not until after a huge screaming fight with William and Lila."

"Followed by a nervous breakdown," Adrienne said. "She moved home with her parents. I heard she went to college eventually."

I was speechless. Why would a successful young dancer do something like that?

"No one talks about it," Zif said, rising to his feet. He gave Adrienne a hand, and they walked back into the studio. I'd upset them.

"Teresa was drama," Ian whispered. "The company did their best to sweep it under the rug."

"She had a real breakdown?" The story was starting to sink in.

He nodded. "She was one of William's favorites for a while. I don't know exactly what happened, but she wanted a promotion and didn't get one.

That was the girl Allison was talking about in Karina's journal? Her whole life was ballet, like mine.

Karina thought Teresa had everything. We all would have thought she had everything.

"That's the saddest thing I've ever heard," I said.

Ian said, "We're all disposable, remember? Everyone was jealous of her and missed that she was seriously depressed."

I stared at him blankly. What went through Teresa's mind? I could only imagine. What would happen if I didn't get promoted this year, either? I might not even get to dance soloist roles at all anymore. How would I feel then?

For the first time, it occurred to me that I should find Karina. It had only been five years since she'd left the company. I had so many questions. Maybe she had wondered where her diary was all this time. Once I finished reading it, I was going to track her down. I wanted to know how her story turned out.

CHAPTER 13

After I read the last entry, I went to Faye's apartment and told her about the journal. I couldn't keep it in anymore, and thinking about Teresa's story made me crazy.

"You should find Karina," she agreed, offering me a piece of chocolate. "We need some good, sound advice from someone who has been in the trenches."

She was right. "I'm thinking about auditioning for other companies," I confessed. "I don't think my career is going in the right direction anymore."

"What if William finds out?" she asked.

My heart sank as I realized how risky that sounded. If I didn't get a job elsewhere and the artistic staff heard I was looking around, would that jeopardize my current job?

Faye took the journal and sat down on her couch. She read while I sewed a pair of pointe shoes.

"I thought I knew a lot about the dancers, but this is eye-opening, isn't it?" she said without looking up.

The next day, I walked to work with renewed resolve. I wasn't ready to give up.

I noticed a couple kissing in front of the entrance as I approached. The woman drew her arms tighter around the man's neck. I recognized Hilary's bun.

They broke apart, and I realized it was Hilary and Grant. I hurried through the door, feeling like I was slowly falling from the sky.

Allison was in the dressing room and noticed my distress immediately. "Are you OK?" she asked.

It wasn't the time or place to be upset, but I couldn't stop myself. I started crying as I changed my clothes. Allison watched me, concerned.

Hilary came in a minute later. "Are you upset?" she asked, seeing my red eyes. The dressing room started filling up, and others glanced over.

My hands were shaking. I picked up my bag and let the door slam as I left the dressing room.

As my fourth season continued, it was like the last three years had never happened. William and Lila seemed to forget I'd been in favor, but I could not. The weeks went by, and going to work became more and more difficult. I cried a lot of the mornings on my walk to work. It was just so hard. I felt humiliated to have fallen so out of favor and disgusted with how bitter and jealous I had become.

I wanted to scream when I saw Hilary rehearse the lead in *Tidal Moods*.

I didn't understand how William and Lila could act as if nothing had changed.

Work was a constant exercise in rage. I began to wish I had never danced any plum roles because now the *corps* parts felt like a letdown. Ballet wasn't a passion anymore; it was my job.

In September, my parents went on a three-month sabbatical to Italy. "It's our second honeymoon," Mom said over the phone. "Don't expect us to call much."

I was so miserable I couldn't be happy for anyone else. Faye noticed my despair and asked persistently why I hadn't tried to find Karina. I told her I didn't have the energy. I wasn't even sure I wanted to hear what she had to say.

During my off-hours, I walked by the house where Ethan dropped a branch on my head. I never saw him, but I fantasized about him and strategized about auditioning for other companies. Artistic directors weren't hiring until January or February, and even though it was early, I made some inquiries about San Francisco, Miami, Seattle, and Boston.

I was scared to go into a new company as an older professional. Despite my problems, I didn't want to leave

William and L.A. I used to have such high hopes for how things would turn out.

At five-thirty, the night before LABT left on an east coast tour, I sat in the back of the studio after I danced my *corps* role in *Fire*. Grant and Hilary rehearsed the *pas de deux*. They were cast to make their debut in upstate New York. The whole scene killed me to watch.

William sat in the front of the studio, his arms crossed, while Hilary danced her solo. I wondered what was going through his mind.

"Deep breath," Faye whispered. It was all I could do not to scream.

I stood and followed Allison on for the finale. I had danced the *corps* in *Fire* so many times I didn't even have to think about it. As I danced, a million thoughts ran through my head. William: "I have big plans for you." Vivienne, my favorite teacher in New York: "Talent means nothing without desire." Jen: "Nothing is fair." My mom: "You feel passionate about things in a way others can't."

All eight *Fire corps de ballet* girls jumped with their right legs extended high. My foot slid out from under me when I landed, and I fell on my left arm. Wasn't this the same way that Karina had broken her leg? My scream was so loud I didn't recognize my voice.

Faye, who was in the second cast and wasn't dancing, drove me to the company doctor while they finished the *Fire* rehearsal. I held an ice bag over my elbow and sobbed in the car. "It's broken. I can tell. There's no way I'm going on the tour. I'm left-handed and couldn't even manage to break my right arm. I won't even be able to wash my hair."

"Everything will be OK," Faye said quietly. She glanced over at me. "You're pretty pathetic, though." She cracked a smile.

I had lost my sense of humor. "Was I that bad in *America?*"

"Bad?" she asked, tightening her grip on the wheel. "Of course not. I thought you were great."

"Why does William hate me now?"

"He doesn't hate you," she said. "There are other dancers that deserve a chance, too. Maybe not Hilary, but one person shouldn't get every role."

"How can I not take it personally?" I asked.

"You just can't," she said. "Look. I realized long ago that I had to shut my eyes to what I didn't want to see if I wanted to last here. You know ballet isn't just satin slippers and curtain calls."

"I used to love ballet so much," I said. "Why am I this miserable?"

The doctor x-rayed my left arm and told me what I already knew. The broken arm would take six weeks to heal. I begged him not to put me in a hard cast, but he said my arm might heal dislocated if I didn't wear it. That meant I'd probably have arthritis when I got older, but if I let him put the hard cast on, my arm would atrophy. It would take twice as long to return to dancing.

My priority was the present, not the future. I couldn't see beyond the current crisis. In ballet, there wasn't later; there was only now. I decided against the hard cast. I was determined to be back in five weeks.

The company left for their two-week tour without me. My dominant arm was useless. My parents were in Italy and didn't know what had happened.

I was all alone.

A few days after my accident, I did the research I'd been avoiding. The address was in Santa Cruz.

I wasn't supposed to drive, but the rolling hills looked open and inviting.

The air was foggy from the coast, and the sleepy feel of the town wrapped around me, comforting and safe. I drove through downtown and headed north, eventually pulling onto a small side street.

"This is it," I said, parking in front of a small gray house with a white picket fence.

I pulled Karina's journal out of my purse and looked at it. She'd been thrilled on the phone. I wasn't sure I was ready to return her book of secrets, but now I had my own story to tell.

The woman who opened the door took my breath away. She was younger-looking than I expected and shockingly beautiful. Tall, with long pitch-black hair, her striking features made her the picture-perfect prima ballerina.

"What happened to your arm?" she asked.

I told her I'd broken it, and the company was on tour.

She beckoned me inside and asked if I wanted a cup of tea—a man called from the kitchen that he would bring out a tray.

I followed her into the living room. Her house felt warm, decorated with plush sofas, cozy blankets, colorful artwork, and a big stone fireplace.

We sat. When I held her diary out, the color drained from her face.

After a minute, she held the journal as if it might break. I watched while she opened the cover.

A man walked in with a platter holding a teapot, tea-cups, and scones. He set the spread down on the coffee table.

"I'm Karina's husband, Rich," he said, shaking my hand. "You should have seen her after you called. You can't imagine what this means to her."

Karina flipped through the pages, lost in thought. Her eyes were watery. Rich poured the tea and handed me a cup. I took mine awkwardly with my right hand and set it down.

"I'm sorry about your arm," he said.

Karina looked up and closed her journal.

I stared at her. "Karina, I read the diary."

Much to my relief, she didn't even blink. "I assumed. Why else would you have found me?"

I breathed a sigh of relief. She was right. I had worried she would be angry. "I'm sorry if I invaded your privacy."

She sucked in her breath. "I would have read it if I were you," she said.

"I have so many questions for you," I blurted out, and as soon as I said it, I started crying.

"Oh, my. It's that bad," Karina said.

"William gave me some big roles," I explained. "Then he lost interest in me."

Karina pursed her lips and shook her head.

"I heard the story about Teresa," I said. "Your journal ends when they cast her in leads, and I wondered what happened. I asked Ian about her, and Adrienne and Zif were there, and they looked like they'd seen a ghost. They told me she had a breakdown. I haven't been able to get her out of my head."

"Nothing changes," Karina said.

"Geez," Rich said, letting out a low whistle. "That place is such a soap opera."

"Karina, why did you finally leave?" I asked.

She glanced at Rich. "Go on," he prompted. "Tell her."

Karina sat for a minute, collecting herself. "I was the one who helped Teresa when she had to contact her parents and quit," she finally said.

I stared at her, trying to imagine. I couldn't.

"We lived on the same block," she said matter-of-factly. "After she didn't show up at work, I stopped by. I'd almost finished my physical therapy and had been starting to take classes again after my injury. I had a spare key because I'd water her plants and stuff when she went home to see her parents in Iowa. She hadn't left her bed for days."

I thought about the times I'd been down and how hard it was to keep going when the world seemed against you.

Karina continued, "A lot of people left after that season. I think fourteen dancers quit. I returned for a few performances, but company life felt suffocating after that time away. I spent that whole year working toward getting back onstage, and when I finally did, it felt empty."

"Why?" I asked.

"I realized how lonely I was, making my whole life about my work," she said. "At the end of the day, it was only ballet. I didn't have a boyfriend or friends outside at all."

My mind went to Ethan. "What did you do?" I asked. "After you left, I mean."

"What most of us do," she said. "I moved back home with my parents for a while. They live in Los Altos. I taught ballet classes at my old studio and started school at Santa Clara. It was the best year of my life. Teaching reminded me why I liked to dance in the first place, and even though college was intimidating, it made me feel hopeful—like there was a future beyond my ballet career. I felt so liberated."

I looked at Rich, seeing how her life expanded after she left the company. "How did you two meet each other?"

"We met in college," Rich said. "She was an undergrad, and I was finishing a master's degree. I was her history professor's assistant." He winked.

I asked Karina, "What do you do now?"

"I'm applying to grad school in psychology and teaching ballet, and Rich is a history professor," Karina said. She put her hand on her belly and smiled. "We're going to be parents in about six months."

For all the wonders my body could do, pregnancy was one I'd never imagined. Her life seemed so full compared with mine.

"Anna," Karina said, her voice changing to a more serious tone, "if you're unhappy, you don't have to stay.

There are many ways to dance without isolating your-self from everything else the world offers. Ballet com-panies have complicated dynamics. You're young, and your family is far away. I know it's scary. Familiar pain over unfamiliar pleasure, as the saying goes. But you're around dancers constantly, exposing you to only one limited worldview."

Her advice took time to digest. The thought of experi-ences beyond my safe, sheltered world terrified me.

"I should get going," I said, checking my watch. "I still have to drive back."

"Will you stay in touch?" Karina asked. "I'd love to hear how you're doing."

We walked to the door and exchanged a hug. Halfway to the car, I stopped and walked back to Karina. She was standing in the doorway watching me.

I said, "I hope you publish your journal. Just write the end first, OK? You have an amazing story."

"It's not all that different from most dancers' stories," she said. "We're all in this together. But I'm glad you got something out of it. That means a lot to me."

When I pulled the car away from the curb, I looked back and watched her gently close her front door. I wondered if someday, I would have a life like hers, with a husband, an education, a house, and a baby on the way. There was no glamour in it, no stage lights, admiring fans, and beautiful costumes.

What would happen to me now? I would go to work when the company returned from tour. I'd hold my head up. I didn't want to leave the way Teresa or Karina did.

When the company returned from tour, I took as much of class as possible with my arm in a sling. I was surprised how much I wanted to move. I missed it. Dancing was what I had always done best, even if I was out of shape. The worst was that everyone felt sorry for me. What I needed was respect, not pity.

William watched me closely. "How are you?" he asked in the back during *grand allegro*.

I wasn't in the mood to talk to him but said I was managing.

He looked thoughtful for a second, then said, "I want you to take your dancing to the next level."

What did he mean?

To my dismay, he moved on without elaborating.

How did he expect me to grow? He and Lila didn't give any specific guidance. There was too much ambiguity: no new roles, no feedback, nothing to challenge me. What they'd given me during my fourth season was the silent treatment.

After a few days back in the studio, my desire faded into bitterness.

By the time *Nutcracker* arrived, I had physically healed. They gave me one show of lead Marzipan. William stood impassively in the front wing while I danced.

The other dancers applauded when I finished, but William walked away. I wasn't even excited to perform anymore. My stage smile had become the ultimate lie.

My fifth-year *corps* contract arrived in the mail at the beginning of March. I signed it without a thought since I had no idea what else I should do and no energy to make changes. I'd been too discouraged and never followed through on my plans to audition elsewhere.

CHAPTER 14

Our final performance of the season was in Palm Springs. I almost felt happy when I went to class on the last day. There were two months of freedom ahead.

I walked to the side of the stage after the *adagio* combination. "Anna," Adrienne whispered behind me.

The second group began the exercise. Adrienne's famous dark eyes met my puzzled expression, and she gave a small indication with her head. William was walking toward me. Others turned to look. It had been a year since I was his favorite. No one expected him to take any notice of me anymore.

He reached me, and the curious faces of the other dancers seemed to melt away. I smelled his familiar cologne when he leaned over. "What are your plans for layoff?" he asked.

I was surprised. "I'm not sure. Take class. Visit my parents, maybe?"

Our eyes met briefly. He turned his head to watch the class. "You need to work on partnering during the layoff," he said. He paused, and I struggled for a response.

"Partnering?" I grew angry. "Where am I supposed to go to work on partnering?"

William said, "That's not my problem, honey."

His words hit me like a blast of cold water in the face. My hands shook, and my voice quivered, but for the first time, I spoke up. "Excuse me, but my name is *not honey*."

He slowly turned around to stare at me, his eyes filled with surprise. My fury had caught him off-guard.

"I can't believe this," he snapped. When our eyes met, I didn't drop my gaze, and he was the one who turned away, shaking his head. He marched to the front of the stage to demonstrate the following combination.

I walked into the wing and picked up my bag. When I glanced back, people were dancing. Ryan, Jeff, and Allison whirled across the floor. Adrienne and Elizabeth whispered in the back. Lorenzo and Grant stood beside each other, arms crossed, and watched. Faye sat, icing her knee in the opposite wing.

No one looked at me. I knew a lot of them had heard my exchange with William. They were pretending not to notice, just like always. Acting was the only way to go on, and I couldn't do it anymore.

I ran downstairs to the *corps* dressing room and locked myself in a bathroom stall. My sobs grew louder as I realized

I was utterly alone. Over the loudspeaker, I could still hear the piano music.

While the company danced above me, I cried so hard my body began to ache. Something inside me needed to explode. William knew everything about how I danced but he didn't know *me*. He didn't know me at all.

I worried through the tech rehearsal that afternoon. Faye asked me what happened with William, and when I told her, she looked at me as if I had committed treason. "No one talks back to him," she said, her eyes opened wide. "What were you thinking?"

My anger from the morning melted under a mountain of fear. I had probably committed professional suicide by asking where I should go to work on partnering. Where *was* I supposed to go?

I hadn't rehearsed any partnered choreography since *America*. Unlike other girls, I didn't have a boyfriend in the company I could ask to practice outside of work hours. There was no school where professional dancers went to practice *pas de deux*.

I should have just nodded and agreed. But I didn't have it in me anymore. Not for him.

And, as William well knew, I had a name.

That evening, when I walked offstage after the first ballet, William seized my arm the moment I passed the wing. I jumped. He pulled me right up to his face. In the darkness backstage, all I could see were his eyes.

"We're going to have words—right now," he said. I followed him into the hall, and he gestured to a small room he used as his office in the theater. When I walked inside, he closed the door.

I was still in the middle of a performance and wasn't yet done for the night. Sweat trickled down my forehead into my eyes. I pulled pins out of my hair. There was less than an hour before I had to go back onstage. I needed to change my hairdo and fix my makeup. He was the last person I wanted to talk to during the show.

When William turned around, he looked surprised to see me working on my hair. "I'm in *Frontiers*," I explained.

"Screw *Frontiers*!" The last thing he cared about at that moment was the performance. I had never seen him like this, and his anger shocked and frightened me.

"You listen here," he said. "If you ever speak to me again the way you did this morning, I'll ask you to leave." He stepped closer to me. My hand fell from my hair, and the pins tumbled. The meeting had nothing to do with my dancing. My relationship with William had finally become personal.

He moved right up in my face, waiting for my response, staring me down.

"I'm sorry, I didn't mean to be rude," I managed, unwanted tears welling in my eyes. My voice came out more desperate than I intended. "Please try to understand. You rarely speak to me. I'm trying so hard to please you. I don't eat. I don't sleep."

"Stop crying," he said. He paced across the room. "I don't want to hear it. Your behavior is inexcusable." He turned back to me, leaned against the far wall, and crossed his arms. We stared at each other.

"I don't mean to make excuses." So, he did care. I stood up tall, gathering my courage. "All I've ever wanted is to dance well for you. You've barely said a sentence to me since last year when you threw me onstage in a huge principal role with only a few days to prepare. After that, you buried me in the *corps* with no explanation. What am I supposed to think?"

He paused and gave me a long look I couldn't read. Then he dropped his arms and let out a burst of laughter. My heart was pounding. He walked over to me and put his hand on my shoulder. Our eyes met.

"Your opinion means everything to me, to all of us," I said. "You gave me opportunities. I did the best I could. Can't you see me as more than just a body? I'm a person, too."

Something in him relaxed. He took a step back. "Maybe I misunderstood."

I let out a sigh. "I have to get ready for *Frontiers*."

He waved his hand dismissively. "OK. Right. Go."

I left the room and ran down the stairs, blood pounding in my ears. As I redid my hair in the dressing room, I decided I didn't want to be looked at on a stage anymore. I needed people to see who I was on the inside.

When I danced *Frontiers* twenty minutes later, William stood in his usual spot in the front wing. I felt his eyes on me and could tell the storm had passed, for him at least. In his mind, everything was about serving the art form. The bigger picture came first, and I was only one person in a much bigger collective effort. His worldview was so much wider than mine. But, I didn't think I'd ever feel the same way about him again. It was the first time I wanted to walk offstage in the middle of my performance.

The season came to an end. Faye and I went to see the new ballet movie, and I recognized the people in it. I wanted to rip the movie poster off the wall when we walked out. Seeing my real life turned into a series of clichés killed me. What happened to those girls after ballet school? No one cared about the consequences.

I started writing in a journal, trying to figure out which direction to go. Then, it was just a matter of finding the courage to follow my heart.

The next time I saw Karina, she put me at ease. We sipped tea. The room smelled like lemon and the fresh roses on the table. Her windows looked out onto the garden. I spoke. She listened.

A month went by. The first day of the season was a week away.

"Anna," my dad said, after endless conversations piecing together my journey and figuring out what was next. "Let's cut to the chase. Time is running out. What do you want to do?"

"I can't talk to William. I'm still too scared." My new calico cat looked at me, turned up her nose, and leaped gently off the bed.

"Forget about William," Mom said. "What do you want to do with your life?"

I was finally mature enough to address this subject beyond the one-liner I'd used for most of my life that reduced me to becoming a dancer and nothing more. New thoughts arrived, ideas I'd only entertained once it dawned on me that life was long and extended outside the ballet studio.

"I want to be more than just a dancer," I said.

My dreams and goals had changed, and I knew I had to find the courage to move on with my life. There was no way I could go back.

At the beginning of September, I called the studios and waited while the secretary directed my call.

William came on the line after several minutes. "I haven't seen you in class over the layoff. Have you been staying in shape? We leave on tour at the end of next month."

I took a deep breath. "I'm calling to tell you I'm not coming back."

There was a long pause. "What?" William said as if there were static on the line. "What was that?"

"I'm starting classes at UCLA for now, and if I still want to by next year, I'll do the audition rounds again. I need to get back to dancing for myself and let ballet be my passion again and not my job. I'm sorry."

He started to say something, then stopped and let out a long sigh. "Are you sure about this?" he asked. "This is a big decision."

"I know how lucky I was to dance for you, but this is right. You don't want me if I don't want to be there. I can't be what you want."

"I see," he said. "We'll miss you."

It hurt to end everything this way.

The line went dead. After a moment, I hung up the phone. I walked to the mirror. My performance was over.

I'd never seen anything more beautiful than the ballet. Maybe ballet was too beautiful. Not enough people appreciated it, and maybe there was a reason. I was learning to accept that humans had flaws, especially me.

My life didn't belong in a work of art anymore. I was the only person who would choreograph how I lived.

The girl I saw in the reflection made my heart ache. Her life was about to fill up with new possibilities. I saw a person who didn't want applause anymore. I wanted to connect with the world in a new and more profound way.

I extended my right arm over my head and pointed my right foot behind my back. My hand came to my heart as I kneeled, bowing my head in a *grande révérance*.

Epilogue

A few months after I left Los Angeles Ballet Theater and started college, I found my way back into a ballet studio for the first time. It was a revelation to discover that I could dance only for myself. My body remembered how much I needed to dance, even if my mind and heart wanted to forget.

To help pay for school, I started teaching fifteen- to eighteen-year-olds at a local ballet school. Watching them, I remembered what I loved about ballet—how the discipline fed our dreams. But the students frightened me with their youthful determination, desire to learn, and almost mystical devotion to the art. How could they know what they were getting into?

The ballet world wasn't terrible—how could it be when I had so many incredible memories and experiences? There were times when I never felt happier to have a calling, a talent, and the ability to give myself joy while I spread it to so many others. But the competitiveness, stress, lack of affirmation, and constant feeling of inadequacy took its toll.

As time passed, I saw how respecting my need for more than ballet was a healthy and life-affirming decision. I even started dating.

Finally, I felt like it was OK to grow up.

My old ballet friends remained an essential part of my life. We had been through something critical that bonded us forever. Over time, the dancers I trained with switched companies, retired, went to college, and found new meaning in their lives. New dancers filled our places.

Nothing inside me died when my ballet career did. I changed.

One rainy Saturday over Thanksgiving break, I caught my reflection in the mirror and realized what I should do.

I sat down at the kitchen table and opened my laptop. My thoughts began to focus as my hands flew over the keys.

"Fifteen minutes. Fifteen minutes, please." The stage manager's voice on the loudspeaker rose over the backstage noise, bringing with it the sounds of the orchestra tuning up and the hum of the audience . . ."

When illusions shatter, someone should tell the story. At this point in my life, I will not be silent. When I think of the young dancers placing their hands on the barre for the first time, I realize it will be up to people like me to pay attention to the individuals. To do the work, dancers need to feel seen, like I did. There will always be struggle and beauty. That won't change. But a life in dance will be easier if we can learn to give more love.

About the Author

© Dan Lao

Miriam Landis is a faculty member at the Pacific Northwest Ballet. She was a LitCamp fellow and an assistant editor at Simon & Schuster, Hyperion, and the Amazon Books team. A Stanford grad, she was also a student at the School of American Ballet and a professional ballerina with Miami City Ballet. When not writing, teaching, or dancing, she enjoys life on Lake Washington alongside her husband and four children. In addition to *Girl on Pointe,* she is the author of *Girl in Motion* and a middle-grade novel, *Lauren in the Limelight.* Learn more at www.miriamlandis.com.

I hope you enjoyed this book. Would you do me a favor?

Like all authors, I rely on community support
and online reviews to encourage future sales.
Your opinion is invaluable. Would you take a few
moments now to share your assessment of my book
on social media and the review site of your choice?
Your opinion will help the book marketplace
become more transparent and useful to all.

As ever,
Miriam

www.ingramcontent.com/pod-product-compliance
Lightning Source LLC
Chambersburg PA
CBHW021159310726
48971CB00002B/701